"I'm sorry about last night," Travis said, **remembering how Callie had melted like hot honey in his arms. "You don't have to worry about it happening again."**

She was going to bolt. He knew it, and rebelled. He didn't want her running away from him.

"Good," she said, and made her move.

He was faster, wrapping his hand around her arm as she stood and turned to leave. Her eyes flashed at his and held, despite the color infusing her cheeks. He waited, watching her blush spread. She didn't pull away, just stood there, a challenge in her eyes, a challenge he couldn't resist.

"You could always have said no, Callie."

Her blush deepened, but she held her ground. Suddenly he was so close to kissing her again, he could feel the warmth of her lips and taste the memory of her mouth. He had an irresistible need to cover her lips with his, to mate with her in any way possible, to claim her. He wanted her to know what this kiss meant, to know what allowing it meant to him.

Callie knew. Her heart pounded with the knowledge. She wanted him. She wanted to be taken by him. The truth was shocking, but inescapable. When he pulled her one step closer, so that every breath he took demanded a breath from her, she was lost. . . .

WHAT ARE *LOVESWEPT* ROMANCES?

They are stories of true romance and touching emotion. We believe those two very important ingredients are constants in our highly sensual and very believable stories in the *LOVESWEPT* line. Our goal is to give you, the reader, stories of consistently high quality that may sometimes make you laugh, sometimes make you cry, but are always fresh and creative and contain many delightful surprises within their pages.

Most romance fans read an enormous number of books. Those they truly love, they keep. Others may be traded with friends and soon forgotten. We hope that each *LOVESWEPT* romance will be a treasure—a "keeper." We will always try to publish

LOVE STORIES YOU'LL NEVER FORGET
BY AUTHORS YOU'LL ALWAYS REMEMBER

The Editors

Glenna McReynolds
A Piece of Heaven

BANTAM BOOKS
NEW YORK · TORONTO · LONDON · SYDNEY · AUCKLAND

*To my dear friend, Betty,
and for Kelly and the cowboys*

A PIECE OF HEAVEN

A Bantam Book / August 1992

If you would be interested in receiving protective vinyl
covers for your Loveswept books, please write to this address
for information:

Loveswept
Bantam Books
P.O. Box 985
Hicksville, NY 11802

ISBN 0-553-44139-6

Published simultaneously in the United States and Canada

PRINTED IN THE UNITED STATES OF AMERICA

OPM   0 9 8 7 6 5 4 3 2 1

One

Travis Cayou dropped his saddle on the floor, then dropped his backside into one of the molded plastic chairs lining the wall of the Laramie, Wyoming, bus station. Damn. He hurt everywhere, bad in the places he hadn't broken, and worse in the places he had.

Rain poured down on the white cinder-block building, streaking the outside of a picture window that framed a muddy Second Street and not much else. Looking around, Travis didn't think the dusty posters tacked to the other three walls gave the wet view much of a run for its money, not at first glance. But he was close to home, and that's what counted. The only thing that counted.

Inhaling deeply and moving in slow motion, he organized himself into the chair. The spurs on his boots jangled a backdrop to his low groan as he stretched his legs out. He took it easy on his right knee, not stretching it too much, just enough to ease a kink or two. The next time some damn bronc decided to kiss the fence, he was getting off first. He swore he would, whether he'd lasted the eight seconds needed to score or not.

Worse yet, he hadn't done any better on his bull ride. That animal had wanted to eat him. He thought he'd ridden every kind of bull that had ever been seen. He'd had them buck and spin so tight, they made their own whirlwind. He'd had them crash beneath him, or worse, try to climb out of the bucking chute with him on their back. But he'd never seen anything like Mad Jack. The next time that particular bovine's number came up with his, he was walking away. He swore he was. They could have his entry fee.

Thinking of which, where in the hell had that clown got off to just before Mad Jack decided to make an hors d'oeuvre out of him? Wasn't that part of what he laid his money down for? For some bullfighting clown to be out there when he dropped his bull rope?

"Heroes," he muttered, wincing at a new pang. Every time some rodeo got a write-up in some newspaper, there was always the same damn headline: "Clowns—Heroes of the Rodeo," or "Clowns—A Bull Rider's Best Friend."

Travis wasn't buying it today. Oh, he'd admit most of them were the hottest things on two legs. Most every time he'd bailed off a bull, one of them had been there to make sure he got out of the arena with all his parts in place. But this last clown had taken one look at old Mad Jack and seen a man-eater. He'd aced Travis in the brains department and kept himself just out of helping distance.

A hero? he thought. Try the cowboy on the back of the raging, bucking beast. The man with the resin smoking on his glove. The man spurring an animal already so fired up he was spitting flames.

The man with more guts than brains. Wasn't that what James had always said?

A wry smile lifted a corner of Travis's mouth. He settled back in the chair and pulled his hat low over his eyes, using his left hand and trying not to jostle his right arm.

He should have been a roper. That's what James had always said. Sure, ropers got hurt sometimes, but more often than not they didn't get stomped all over creation.

His left hand dropped back onto his thigh, making a print in the dust turned to mud on his jeans. Lord, he was tired. He was getting too old to have his tail end kicked by rough stock. He was getting too old to be following the rodeo circuit with only half his heart in it. He made enough to pay expenses and keep his checkbook from rolling over in a dead faint, and that was about it.

His wrist hurt like hell. The doctor had given him some pain pills, real good stuff. But how many times could a man break the same damn wrist in the same damn place and expect it not to hurt all the time, mended or not?

Probably not many, Travis decided, digging in his shirt pocket for another painkiller. At least it was a clean break this time. He swallowed the pill dry, too tired to get up and fight the rain for a can of pop from the machine outside.

He was finished. He swore he was. It was time for him to go home. Hell, it was long past time for him to go home. He'd done eight years of penance. He was tired of running from James's memories and his own guilt.

James was the one who'd married Beth Ann. He was the one who'd brought her up to their ranch on the Colorado side of the Colorado-Wyoming border.

He was the one who had left her alone day after day, and sometimes night after night, while he wheeled and dealed. All Travis had done was try to help her over the rough spots, and if he'd wanted to do more, well, he hadn't done nearly as much as she'd begged him to do.

But the past was over. It was time for him to go home and lay claim to his half of the Cayou Land and Cattle Company. Ranching was a way of life, and Travis wanted his life back, the life he'd been born to live. He missed the scent of sage on the evening breeze. He missed watching the sun sliding into the Rockies. He missed the quiet. The same quiet that had driven Beth Ann to acts of desperation.

She'd hated it all, the wild silence waiting outside the confines of the ranch buildings, the snow-capped peaks penning her in. It was a hell of a life for a woman, but his mother had done it. Hell, lots of women could do it, if their men took care.

One thing he knew for sure, the Cayou Land and Cattle Company needed a woman's touch. He'd stopped by three years ago when he'd known James would be at the National Western Stock Show, and the house had looked run-down and worn-out, not at all like home, not at all the way his mother had kept it. Even Beth Ann had done better. Shoat, one of the old-timers at the ranch, had told him then that he ought to come home, that the ranch needed him.

Well, he was coming home now, busted up, road weary, and saddle sore.

Hell, *he* could use a woman's touch, Travis thought. He shifted in his chair and grimaced against the pain. Someone sweet and willing, soft and well rounded. Someone warm. Someone with good hands.

He slid farther down, resting his head on the back

of the chair and holding on to his casted right forearm. *Yeah, someone with good hands.*

He smiled as he closed his eyes and readjusted his hat against the weak gray light coming in through the window. Woman, hell. What he needed was sleep. Shoat had said it would take him at least an hour, maybe two, to get to the bus station from the ranch. Then he'd be heading home to stay. Providing James didn't try to kick him back out again.

Travis let out a weary sigh. If James did try, he was going to find a fight on his hands, and not one of those knock-down, drag-out, wrestle-in-the-dirt kind of fights they'd had over Beth Ann eight years ago. He'd backed off then, because of a guilt he still wasn't sure was his to bear. He wasn't backing off this time, not an inch.

He needed to go home, and he'd do whatever he had to, whatever it took to get him there and make it stick. Nobody or nothing was going to stop him.

Callie Michael fought her way through the storm into the bus station, slamming the door behind her and shutting out the wind-whipped rain. She stood on the old beige carpet, dripping one puddle beneath her boots and another one a few inches out, where the rain ran down and off the rolled brim of her hat.

The storm was quickening up, threatening to turn into one of the year's best, especially up north and in the mountain ranges to the west. Luckily, she was heading southwest, back to Colorado, back to the Cayou Land and Cattle Company, she and James's little brother.

She wiped a palm up her cheek and shook the water off her fingers, her gaze steady on the lone occupant of the waiting area. He didn't look all that little.

Six foot plus of cowboy lay sprawled over a short bank of chairs, one arm flung out like a rag doll's, the other cradled close to his chest in a sling and a cast. Long legs, a hard-sided suitcase, an Association saddle, and a rigging bag draped with the fanciest chaps Callie had ever seen took up a good third of the floor space on the customer side of the counter. It wasn't Travis Cayou's white and gold chaps with the silver lightning bolts that held her gaze, though.

His jeans had been split from ankle to hip on his right leg, and the first aid tape that was supposed to hold them together was giving up with the wet and the dirt. As a rule, cowboys didn't go around showing off their legs, and Callie figured Travis Cayou didn't either. His leg was a color closer to the white bandage wrapped around his knee than it was to the darkly tanned skin of his large, square hands.

Strong hands. The thought crossed her mind and momentarily caught her attention. His hands were the essence of strength, rugged and weather-worn, built of sinew and bone and brought to life by the ridges of veins tracking beneath his skin. She would have expected no less. Every working cowboy needed strong hands. Someone who bet his life on the ability of five fingers to hold him onto half a ton of bucking bronc or a ton of aggravated bull needed more than a strong hand. He needed an arm of steel to back it up.

Her gaze slipped up the pearly snaps on his cream-colored shirt, taking in the streaks of mud and the dirt ground into the cloth. His head was tilted back against the small chair, giving him plenty of snoring room. A day's growth of sandy beard darkened the chin and jaw jutting out from beneath the black Stetson that covered his face. She noted the small bandage taped high on his cheek-bone, and the bit of blood showing on the gauze wrapped around his knee. From the looks of him, he'd taken more than one spill last night. No wonder Shoat had been worried about him.

Finally, her gaze settled on his right hand, half hidden by the cast. He was loosely cupping the big gold and silver rodeo buckle at his waist, as if he were trying to hold whatever was left of himself together.

An unconscious sigh lifted her chest. Her glance drifted to his saddle and his rigging bag and those fancy chaps, then back to him. He was a wreck, but he looked mostly like what he was, a saddle tramp, the prodigal son returning home, a cowboy on the short end of the rodeo circuit. What he did not look like was James's brother, let alone James's little brother.

James wasn't six foot of anything, and he sure didn't have legs like that—long, lanky, and put together in a way that made her gaze stray back to the mostly naked bandaged one. Ropes of muscle corded his thigh and his calf, flexing with every slight movement he made in his sleep. It was a sight to see, and it made Callie's mind wander in unaccustomed ways.

She blushed at her sensual musing, then became irritated with herself. She'd obviously been cooped up with Shoat and the cows too long if she was ogling the likes of Travis Cayou. He was no business of hers. She'd only come as a favor to Shoat, and she hoped to hell James never found out she'd done even that much. Her boss was darn touchy when it came to his younger brother.

Quietly clearing her throat, she forced her gaze to the bus station clerk. The red-haired lady was doing the same thing she'd been doing, staring at more man than either of them was used to seeing. It was ridiculous.

"Mr. Cayou? In from Colorado and New Mexico?" she asked, gesturing with her thumb and drawing the clerk's attention.

"Yeah." The clerk grinned. "He's been kind of decorating up the lobby this afternoon. You got here in the nick of time. I was about to close up. Figured I'd just take him home with me." The grin broadened, taking half a dozen years off the older woman's face, and leaving no doubts in Callie's mind about what the lady had been planning to do with him. From what she'd heard about Travis Cayou, he drew women like a lodestone—whether they were married or not.

She gave him another inadvertent glance. At least now she knew why. He had a look about him, and she hadn't even seen his face.

But that wasn't her problem. Her problem was getting him home.

She took a step toward him, then hesitated, feeling a tingle of wariness, or shyness, speed up her pulse. Chastising herself for more foolishness, she wiped her hand across her middle and took the last two steps to him, her boots squishing softly on the carpet.

"Mr. Cayou?" She reached out and touched him lightly on the shoulder. "Mr. Cayou?"

From a far-off distance, Travis heard a husky sweet voice calling him. He debated with himself whether it was worth waking up, whether it was worth coming back to all of his aches and pains to find out who was behind the coaxing voice. But it

wasn't much of a debate, especially when she repeated his name louder and gripped his shoulder
tighter to give him a shake.

"Mr. Cayou? Travis? Come on, wake up, Travis."

The increased contact helped him slip closer to
consciousness and sent home an instinctively
known fact: She had good hands. He could feel the
warmth of them, the gentle pressure, the just-right
touch. She was probably good with horses. In the
haziest of thought processes, he wondered if she'd be
good with him, this lady whose voice he wished was
whispering a little closer to his ear, this lady whose
voice he'd like to hear with more need straining the
sweetness, a more passionate need.

"Travis? Come on, wake up. Shoat sent me to
bring you home."

Passion. Lord it had been a long time, and never
with a woman with a voice like a hot summer night,
soft but laced with a husky edge. He needed to meet
this lady. Seems old Shoat had sent him a woman
right out of his dreams, even if she did sound a mite
on the impatient side.

Drawing in a deep breath and wishing he'd taken
another pain pill, he dragged himself up from his
deep sleep. Slowly, he lifted his hand and pushed his
hat to the back of his head.

Callie had been ready for anything—anything except the hard reality of Travis Cayou. In the space of
a few seconds, the time it took for him to lift his hat,
he went from being a half-infirm, broken down,
physically intriguing cowboy to the most hazardous
material in Wyoming, unsafe at any speed.

From under the brim of the black Stetson, barely
focused eyes of the darkest brown stared at her. His
gaze trailed over her face in a slumberous caress,
leaving a path of sudden, unwelcome heat on her

skin. As her cheeks flushed, a rawly sensual smile formed on his mouth.

How something moving so slowly could have the impact of a speeding freight train was beyond her, but she felt shaken to the toes of her boots by the implicit sexuality of his smile. Heat raced through the rest of her body, touching her everywhere and pooling in liquid warmth in her veins.

She swallowed hard and took a half step backward, stumbling slightly over her boot heel. He was making a thousand promises with his smile and with the midnight fires banked in the depths of his eyes, the kind of promises most women dreamed about and most men couldn't keep. He was also sending messages. One in particular was loud and clear: He wanted to take her to bed, right now. She'd never had it said to her any plainer, and she'd never felt herself react to the invitation with such an electrifying physical response.

Travis did want to take her to bed, every inch of her, from the wild ebony hair escaping her hat and her braid, to the generous curves of her breasts, to the slim-hipped elegance of her long legs. But he didn't have the wherewithal to do anything but think about it, because fast on the tracks of consciousness came pain, dull and heavy and inescapable. His fantasy and his smile both took the short, downward slide into the truth. He thought about saying hello, but the pain told him to do something else.

Grimacing, he dropped his hand to his pocket and dug out the brown plastic bottle filled with his pain pills. He took two and closed his eyes on an unsolicited groan.

Callie's heart lurched. Raw sex was a bit beyond her ability to handle, but nurturing was well within her acceptable guidelines for personal or even impersonal relationships. Taking care of cows was what she did for a living.

She took the bottle out of his hand and read the label. Her eyebrows slowly rose as she looked back at him, and once again he took her by surprise, just by being there and looking the way he did.

He was a lot younger than James, maybe ten years younger, yet he was harder looking, as if life hadn't settled as easily on him. Sandy-brown hair streaked with blond framed a lean, handsome face set off by a short nose and square chin with a slight cleft, a face tanned by the sun and chiseled by a life spent as a range rider and a rodeo cowboy.

Callie had never been anywhere to speak of, but she was pretty sure they didn't make men like him anyplace on earth except east of the Pacific Ocean and west of the Mississippi River, and he was a rare breed even there. He was the kind of man she'd grown up knowing, a cowboy, but no cowboy she'd ever met had made her blush.

Her cheeks warmed again. He was good-looking all right, in a rugged, impish way, and his smile ought to be against the law, at least in public, but it was obvious to anyone she could outrun him in his present condition.

"We better get you into the truck while you can still walk," she said, putting the pills in her own pocket. By her count and the instructions on the bottle, he'd had more than enough.

"Who said I can walk?" he asked softly, his eyes still closed, his face still tight with pain.

"I'll take your saddle and your gear out, give you a few minutes for those pills to take the edge off." She stepped around his legs, her wet duster slapping against her jeans.

"Wait a minute." Travis opened his eyes a fraction of an inch and tried to move when he saw her lift his saddle, but his body wasn't obeying. "Hey, wait a minute. Who are you?"

The dark-haired angel in the white canvas duster and black cowboy hat turned and leveled on him the most startlingly blue gaze he'd ever seen.

"Kathleen Ann Michael. I work at the ranch. You can call me Callie." She turned again to leave.

"I had a mare named Calliope once. We called her Callie for short. Smartest horse I ever owned," he said, then immediately wished he hadn't, but it had been the first thing to come to mind. Well, actually, the second thing. First had been the word "pretty," as in "real pretty," so pretty he felt his gut tighten just looking at her.

Those aquamarine eyes slanted him a purely innocent glance over her shoulder. "Yeah, well, I used to have a dog named Travis, but he wasn't exactly on the bright side." She paused as if considering her words, then added, "We didn't keep him around for his looks, either."

Travis wasn't sure if he'd been insulted or not. Either way, he couldn't stop his grin. "He must have had some good points."

"A couple," she agreed, hefting the saddle higher in front of her, holding on to it with both hands.

Travis tried to rise, but she stopped him with a quelling look.

"I can carry your saddle, your suitcase, and your rigging bag, but I can't carry you. So do us both a favor and save your strength."

The angel had spoken. Travis collapsed back in the chair to wait his turn. If he'd had any confidence whatsoever about his ability to get out the door on his own, he would have helped her. But spending the afternoon cramped in the little chair had stiffened him up something terrible. Parts of him were even starting to shake.

At first he tried to ignore it, but by the time she carried his suitcase out, his knee was knocking against the chair, an added pain he really didn't need.

He gripped his right thigh with his left hand and tried to massage the spasm out of the muscles. He wished he'd dropped his bull rope two seconds later than he had the previous night. The extra time would have gotten him to the eight-second horn and might have put him down someplace other than under the bovine tornado.

He wished the pills would kick in too. Pressing his palm harder into his thigh, he worked the muscle with his thumb and fingers. And if he was going to fall apart like this, he wished Shoat had come himself instead of sending Kathleen Ann Michael.

The sound of the door slamming brought his head up quick. Just as quickly, he looked back down at his leg. There were lots of things he liked getting from women. Pity wasn't one of them.

"Should I be taking you over to the hospital before we go home?" she asked.

"No." He pressed even harder on his leg, willing the muscles to relax, and they did. Slowly at first, then deeply. A sense of well-being began infusing his senses. "Callie, I . . . I think we better get me into the truck. Real quick."

Callie didn't need to be told twice. She was at his side in three strides, wrapping his good arm around her neck and sliding her arm around his waist. "I've got you. On three. One—"

"I'll be glad to help you, honey," the station clerk offered, coming around from behind the counter.

Callie just bet she would, and if the lady had helped her with his gear, she might have considered it. As it was, she was determined to get him out on her own, all six feet of him. Six feet of lean muscle, long legs, strong arms, and rock-hard body.

"No, thanks. I've got him," she said, indulging in a small lie. He was all over her and slipping fast, but the red-haired lady wasn't going to lay a hand on him, not if Callie had anything to say about it. He belonged to her outfit, and she was the boss, the foreman of the home ranch of the Cayou Land and Cattle Company. Nobody was going to call her shots for her.

Not even you, Travis Cayou. She stiffened her resolve and one knee and shifted her shoulder deeper under his arm, trying to take more of his weight and inevitably ending up with her right side mashed up against his left side. He half groaned, half sighed in response.

Normally, she wouldn't have noticed. After all, she was only helping a hurt man out to the truck. But that hurt man was Travis Cayou, and when his hat brushed up against hers and his pained sigh echoed in her ear, she couldn't ignore the warm blush blooming on her cheek, the catch in her throat, or the resulting shiver winding its way down her spine.

She would have dropped him right then and there, like a hot skillet, if it hadn't meant more work to get him back up. For a moment she tried to blame her reaction on skipping lunch, but she'd skipped more than one meal in her life without going all hot and cold in the middle of the afternoon.

"You all right?" she asked in a voice meant to be

gruff. It sounded provocative instead, even to her own ears.

"I'll make it," was all he said, very softly, very close, his arm tightening around her shoulders.

Callie swore soundlessly and headed him out the door.

Two

The wipers slapped back and forth across the windshield, scraping off the rain and sleet. With her luck, Callie figured they'd end up in a blizzard long before they got back to the ranch. She hoped Shoat and the new hand had gotten all the heavy heifers cut out and moved to the calving pens. Shoat was the best cow man on the border, but the new man was still an unknown quantity. Lately, sober help had been hard to find, and good help darn near impossible.

Her glance strayed to the man sound asleep and propped up in the seat beside her. From everything James had told her, she doubted if he'd be much help. At this point, though, she'd settle for not having another hindrance to handle. Shoat seemed to have more faith in the younger Cayou, but Shoat had a soft spot for all of life's wild ones. Travis Cayou was definitely one of the wild ones.

Four years back he'd been the champion bareback rider at Cheyenne Frontier Days. There had been a big write-up in the Laramie paper about the hometown boy from across the border, complete with pictures. But all of the pictures had shown only his winning form on the back of a bronc, hat jammed low, chaps flying, free hand raised high. None of them had shown him with that smile on his face.

An irritated sigh escaped her. She knew just enough about men to know when to stay away from one, and Travis Cayou was absolutely one she needed to stay away from. She was surprised she even had to tell herself. He was pure trouble. If James's stories hadn't been enough to convince her, Travis's smile sure was.

She flipped on her blinker and turned the truck onto a less-traveled highway.

His coming home was bound to upset the apple cart, reason enough to resent him in her book. She'd just gotten things worked out with James where he trusted her enough to let her in on some of the major decisions concerning her end of the CLC.

Whatever upset was going to happen, though, would have to wait until James got back from his business trip. He hadn't exactly confided the details of his business or the purpose of his going East to talk to a bunch of New Yorkers and such, but if it affected the home ranch, he was bound to tell her when he returned. Until then she'd put Travis up in the main house and hope he didn't need too much looking after, because she sure didn't have the time or the inclination to look after him.

She needed another nightrider to get her through calving, someone who noticed things. She'd lost two calves the previous night because Bill Webster hadn't noticed much beyond his liquor bottle. Bill Webster was looking for another job.

The sleet did its final transformation into snow, and Callie swore under her breath. She was in for a long, wet, cold night.

Travis heard the soft cussing and opened his eyes. He felt better, almost human. The medication was working on his body without messing too much with his mind. Oh, he felt a little woozy, but it was pleasant without being disorientating.

Another quiet curse floated through the air. He tilted his head back into the corner of the cab to get a better view of her. She was gorgeous. Windblown, wet, and gorgeous, and she worked on his ranch. Shoat was right. He should have come home a long time ago.

"Quite a storm we're heading into," he said, watching her for the sheer pleasure of it.

She nodded and leaned forward to tap her knuckle against the gas gauge. He saw the needle waver up around the full mark. She settled back into the seat.

"Have you been at the ranch long?" he asked, making another stab at conversation.

"Awhile." She rolled the window down and adjusted the side mirror, giving a darn good impression of someone trying to ignore him. Since they'd just met, he could think of only one reason for her to be so inclined, and one person to get her that way.

What was James up to? he wondered. Did this woman belong to him? Or was she just part of the ranch?

They'd never had a hired woman before, but surely Shoat would have tracked him down somewhere and told him if James had gotten married again.

Another woman of James's. He tried the label in his mind, still looking at Callie. He didn't like it. He didn't like it at all.

He told himself she didn't look like James's type, nothing like the outwardly prim and proper Beth Ann. James's ex-wife had honey blond hair, thick and soft, not like the wild mane of black curls Callie

Michael had tried to restrain in a long, fancy braid. French braid, he thought they called it. A lot of the women on the circuit wore their hair the same way. He liked the style.

He especially liked it on her, the way the shiny hair swept up and away from her cheek, leaving a few tendrils dampened in a vee against her softly tanned skin. He had the craziest, sincerest urge to lean over and taste her with his tongue. Maybe slide his mouth down the side of her neck, kissing her, laving the tender skin, and sinking himself knee-deep in the sensations he knew awaited him there.

He wanted to kiss her mouth. He didn't try to hide the truth from himself—the yearning was too real— but he did figure it was in his best interests not to let her know how she was affecting him. From what he'd seen in the bus station, she was the skittish type. That didn't bother him. He'd always liked the chase, the give and take, the pause and parry before sur- render. But there was every possibility he was way out of line thinking about kissing her—if she be- longed to James.

Lord, he hoped she didn't. His luck had been running bad, but nobody's luck could run that bad. Could it?

"Thanks for coming in to get me," he said. "I expected Shoat." A part of him still wished Shoat had come. He'd felt like a fool watching a woman load up his gear.

"Shoat can't handle driving on bad roads any- more. He says his reflexes are shot."

Shoat had been saying that for over twenty years, by Travis's reckoning. Seems the old man had finally found somebody who believed him. He wasn't about to disillusion her, but he remembered a time when Shoat had driven him home from a Little Britches rodeo in Steamboat Springs, through the worst blizzard of the decade. They were the only vehicle to get over Rabbit Ear's Pass in a forty-eight-hour stretch, and the only thing to get over Cameron Pass that entire week. Shoat had complained about his reflexes being shot the whole way.

Must do the old buzzard's heart good, Travis thought, to have somebody as pretty as Callie listening to his complaints for a change.

A few freckles dusted the bridge of her nose, but they didn't detract from the overall elegance of her profile. She had enough eyelashes for three people, and they were a thick fringe around her incredible eyes. The color of her eyes was beautiful, unique, but that wasn't what made him notice them. It was the glint of steel in there amongst all the pretty aquamarine. Travis found it fascinating, like her voice, soft and tough at the same time.

No, he decided firmly, she wasn't like Beth Ann. That lady had been all soft and no tough, except when it came to getting what she wanted, which eight years ago had included him.

He'd learned a few things since then about older women who liked playing with younger men, and no woman could get away with doing to him what she'd gotten away with. She'd strung him along, teased him to distraction and beyond, made promises she didn't keep and demands he'd had enough sense to back away from. In the year she and James were married, he'd gone from being in awe of the beautiful woman his brother had brought home, to half in love with her, to disgust. It was a wonder James hadn't shot them both.

He'd tried of course, the night he'd caught them all over each other in her bedroom, but he'd missed. Knowing his brother's skill with a firearm, Travis had taken it as fair warning and had tried to stay away from Beth Ann. She'd had other ideas, though, chasing him all over the ranch until James had caught them again with her doing things she ought not have been doing and Travis having no luck at all stopping her.

James hadn't bothered with the gun that time, but sent Travis flying with a right cross and an uppercut. His gaze strayed back to Callie. Either his brother's taste had improved greatly over the years, or Callie Michael wasn't the new wife.

She couldn't be a new wife, he stubbornly insisted to himself.

"You married?" he asked.

She glanced over at him, then back at the road. "How's your knee?"

"Hurts."

"And your arm?"

"The arm is fine, but the wrist hurts like hell."

"I'm going to put you up in the main house."

"That'll work out pretty good," he drawled, shifting his bandaged leg into a more comfortable position. "Considering that's where my room is."

"Shoat usually starts supper about three or three-thirty," she continued, ignoring the hint of humor in his voice. "If you can manage your own breakfast and lunch, it would be a great help."

"I'm a big boy," he said, his voice holding the same ironic tone.

"Yeah, well, it's calving season, and I'm a little shorthanded."

"But are you married?"

Callie looked over at him, and a slow smile curved his mouth, an easy, natural smile, not the thousand-volt one meant to melt a woman's sense, but a fairly potent one nonetheless. She considered herself fore-warned and prayed the warning stuck.

"Not married," she answered, downshifting for the bad stretch of road up ahead.

Travis's prayers had been answered. If she'd been married to James, he'd have been tempted to say to hell with coming home and just had her turn the truck back toward Laramie. A man could only take so much of fate twisting his life around. He and James had hardly ever agreed on anything in thirty years. To have twice fallen for the same woman would have been too much.

He watched her while she drove on through the falling snow and fading light. Her fingers absently tapped an unheard rhythm on the steering wheel, the sound silenced by the tawny leather gloves she wore. Every now and then she checked the rearview mirror, giving him a glimpse of a graceful throat above the collar of her duster and the red and black plaid scarf wrapped around her neck.

She had a real pretty mouth, not full or pouty, or overly curved. It looked softly sweet, like it could get the job done and then some.

And then some . . . His gaze drifted from her mouth to her eyes and back again. The longer he looked at her, the easier it was to fantasize about kissing her, about tasting her and feeling her soften in his arms.

A sensation other than pleasantness started working on him, the edgy beginnings of arousal. He was surprised at how easily she stirred him. All she'd done was call his name in his sleep and he'd wanted her. For a long time he'd made a habit of not wanting what he shouldn't have or couldn't handle, and beautiful, wild women had been at the top of his list.

Looking at her, he decided that maybe it was time to reorganize his list.

They rode in silence for the next few miles. Callie tried to think about cows and not about the man in the seat next to her, barely far enough away. Thinking about him made her nervous. Of course, it was probably only natural for her to be nervous around the man who owned half of the ranch where she was the foreman, especially when he didn't know she was his foreman.

She was pretty sure he couldn't fire her. James had hired her and promoted her, and what with him being off the ranch more and more, she was definitely needed. Even if Travis turned out to be a fair hand, she'd still be needed. Unless, of course, he brought in his own people.

Where he'd find them was beyond her. She'd been looking high and low for the two hands she needed and had only come up with one twenty-year-old kid, Pete Rankin. She'd have to do better at roundup and haying time. She knew what they said about rodeo cowboys—"Too proud to cut hay and not quite wild enough to eat it."

Well, if Travis was still there when the hay came in, he'd better be able to leave his pride back at the house and get himself into the fields. The Hammond boys had hired out the year before, but she'd had to spend too much time riding herd on the younger ones.

According to James, the young Hammond boys weren't the only people who needed riding herd on. He'd told her he'd spent half his growing years trying to corral his little brother and keep him out of trouble. At the time, he'd had a wistful smile on his face. Of course, he'd been a little on the drunk side. Whenever he got more than a little on the drunk side, which was rarely, his wistfulness disappeared. James was a mean drunk, and Callie had learned early on how to stay out of his way.

There hadn't always been bad blood between the brothers, but Shoat had told her things had gone downhill fast after Beth Ann came to the ranch. He hadn't said much else. He hadn't needed to; Callie had figured the rest of it out on her own. Two men and one woman could easily spell trouble.

She'd put Travis up in the main house and that would be the end of it. He was James's problem. And as far as the blushing business went, well, the novelty of having this rugged, broad-shouldered, good-looking rodeo cowboy around the place was bound to wear off before the week was out. She'd just been cooped up with Shoat and the cows too long.

Travis was riding quietly, conserving his energy, allowing his fantasies free range, and hoping his medication lasted all the way to the ranch. He seemed to have misplaced his pills and was in for a long night if he didn't find them.

The pavement gave way to graded dirt and road base at exactly the same place it always had, but the sudden jostling caught him unprepared and sent pain lancing through his knee.

The first word out of his mouth wasn't one he usually used in front of women. Neither was the second, or the third. He wound down with "dammit," then went on to add a word he'd used with women a lot a few years back.

"Sorry." Sorry, as in "I never meant to hurt you." Sorry as in "Can we still be friends?"—until he'd realized his friendship was just more heartache to the ones who'd really cared.

"You didn't bust anything open, did you?" she asked, nonplussed by his language.

"No. I think the doctor sewed me up pretty good," he said as casually as he could muster, considering his knee had just about spontaneously combusted on him.

"What happened?"

"I got lucky on the draw," he said, knowing she was asking about his wreck in the arena.

She didn't answer, concentrating on turning the steering wheel with both hands and maneuvering the truck onto a narrow road, under the stone arch declaring the Cayou Land and Cattle Company.

He was home. He'd been so busy watching her, he hadn't watched the landscape, the country sweeping past. He watched it now, and with every rise of hill, with every curve in the river, his heart tightened.

Cottonwoods lined the banks of the Laramie, giving way to willows in the meadows. The water ran clear, clean, and cold, built by the freshets and streams winding down from the mountains. Spring wasn't quite there yet. The pastures weren't quite green, and a dusting of snow covered all the land, but it was home, the earth and sky of his childhood, his young manhood, and his dreams.

"Get anything rode?" she asked, drawing his attention back to her.

"The bareback bronc. I won top money. But the saddle bronc scraped me off on the fence in about five seconds, and the bull lost me in about six."

"My dad was a bull rider."

"Oh, yeah?" He grabbed onto the common ground. "What's his name?"

"I don't know."

He stared at her for a minute, silenced by the unexpected revelation. "Why?" he asked finally, his voice rough with emotions stronger than he'd realized. "Why don't you know?"

She glanced at him, then returned her gaze to the road. After a moment she said, "Because my mom didn't ever want me running after a man who didn't have enough guts to stick around in the first place."

Travis continued staring at her, home forgotten, until she pulled up to the ranch house and stopped the truck. When she started to get out, he reached for her and laid his hand on her arm, holding her.

She turned and looked at him over her shoulder. The yard light caught the darkened color of her eyes and cast a shadow from the brim of her hat across her face. She was beautiful, her face framed by the soft wool of her scarf, her braid a serpent of dark silk across the white canvas of her duster.

He wanted to say he was sorry. Sorry for what a man he'd never known had done. But when he looked into her eyes, the words lodged in his throat.

This woman didn't want his platitudes, his excuses, and he didn't want to give them to her. He didn't want his ties to her to be sullied by somebody else's mistakes.

"Thanks," he said softly, releasing her. "Thanks for bringing me home."

Callie didn't have a reply, but one wasn't needed. She shifted her glance and saw Shoat coming down the porch steps.

She never tired of returning to the ranch. The home place of the CLC was like something out of a picture book. The low-slung ranch house sat amidst an encompassing grove of aspens, dappled by sunlight during the day and caressed by the wind soughing through the trees at night. Age-darkened logs chinked with white rose from a foundation of Morrison sandstone. The original homestead was the foyer of the current house, a remembrance of Cayous past, of the generations of men and women who had tamed the borderland and made it their own.

"Travis!" the old man called, holding on to the rail, his bow legs skinny as a crow's. "Travis!"

Between the two of them, she and Shoat got Travis into the house and settled in his room. He'd wanted to sit around in the kitchen awhile, but Shoat had taken one look at him and decreed bed rest.

"I told you, boy. I told you a thousand times to stay off them sonuvabees. 'Scuse me, Callie." Shoat fussed around his new charge, bringing a smile to the younger man's face.

"A man's got to eat, Shoat." Travis let himself be sat down, propped up, and generally taken care of.

"Sure, boy. I'm always one for eating, got nothin' against it. But looks to me like all you've been eating is dirt, and getting more than your share."

Travis laughed, and Callie caught the shadow of pain cross his face. His good arm tightened around his rib cage. She looked at Shoat, but he was busy jamming Travis's clothes into the dresser, as if he was afraid the "boy" might get up and walk out.

Her gaze settled back on Travis, their eyes meeting. "Is there anything you *didn't* break?" she asked.

He winced and looked up at her. Then, unbelievably, he grinned again.

"I've got a couple of parts still in good working order." A teasing light glimmered in his eyes, and sure enough, she blushed.

"Shoat," she said. "I'm going down to get my supper. How did Pete Rankin do today?"

Shoat turned around, holding a stack of shirts. "Good. Real good. The boy's got plenty of cow sense, and he knew enough to let Babe do the cutting. Darn good horse, that Babe."

"How's it going at Reese Park and Connor's

Place?" Those were the other two Cayou ranches, and she knew the foremen of each would have checked in with Shoat sometime during the day.

Connor's Place reminded her the most of the home ranch, backed up as it was against the mountains. The ranch house was smaller, but they ran a bigger herd than she did. Reese Park, though, was a whole 'nother ball game, lying farther to the south and east, and taking up its share of northern Colorado. Miles of prairie stretched over low-lying hills and the occasional bluff. The North Fork of the Cache la Poudre River ran through it, offering some of the best fishing anywhere. Forest blanketed its western boundary, and she'd chased her share of cows through those trees. Mostly, though, Reese was grass, thousands of acres of buffalo grass, to grow cattle on and to make a living on.

"They're doing good," Shoat said. "I've got all the figures on the desk for James when he gets back, but the Lord knows I ain't no bookkeeper. You ought to look it all over. Kyle said he's got an elk herd feeding off one of his hay stacks at Reese. I told him to send us some fresh venison."

Travis was following the conversation and getting a general idea about Callie Michael's work on the ranch. She was one of the hands, not the cook, not the housekeeper, not the bookkeeper. She worked out, meaning outside, and not meaning anything to do with weight machines and aerobics.

James had not only hired himself a woman, he'd hired a woman ranch hand. He hadn't figured his brother for the liberated type.

"That's between you and Kyle," Callie answered Shoat. "Does Pete know he's working with me to-night?"

"I cut him loose at noon for him to grab a bite and

get some sleep. He was looking a little peaked earlier, but the boy's young. He'll be fresh as a daisy for you."

Shoat was wrong. By the time Callie had eaten her supper and found Pete in the bunkhouse, he'd already lost his own supper and was running a temperature near the hundred-degree mark.

She fixed him up as best she could and swore all the way to the barn. She hadn't planned on being the sole nightrider for this cow and calf outfit for the rest of the season. She'd hired Pete Rankin for that job. All she'd needed was to work with him, make sure he knew what he was doing, and she'd go back to sleeping at night. Or at least go back to sleeping until she was needed to help with a difficult birth.

The two-year-old heifers in the south pasture were her responsibility. She didn't like losing a single calf to carelessness, but everyone on her cow crew was working fourteen-hour days and overlapping shifts. She'd been at Reese Park her first year, before she'd been moved to the home ranch to work under Shoat. The big herds were still north, at Reese and Connor, but she and Shoat had the fewest losses. This being her first year as the foreman, she'd be damned if she'd lose the record.

In the barn she saddled one of her horses, a bay gelding with the disposition of a saint. Given her present mood, she could only hope they balanced each other out and met somewhere in the middle.

She stopped at her small house and changed into long johns and a pair of down-filled coveralls for the night's work. It was then she remembered Travis's pain pills. The bottle poked out of the pocket of the shirt lying on the bed, giving her a guilty twinge. The man was in no shape to face the night without his medication.

She looked down at her blood-and-muck-stained coveralls. Miraculously she'd managed to get them washed earlier in the morning, but the stains were permanent. She didn't even bother to swear.

Grabbing his pills and pulling a stocking cap on her head, she stomped out of her house. She had a delivery to make before heading up to the calving sheds, and she was going to make it in her absolute worst set of rags. One thing for sure, though, she doubted if he could make her blush in her calving coveralls.

She should have known better. He had her blushing before she even got inside the main house.

Three

Callie's hand stilled on the back porch rail, then gripped hard as her boot slipped and slid partway across an icy step. She righted herself and peered again across the porch, through the back door window and into the kitchen. Damn him. What in the hell did he think he was doing? Hadn't Shoat put him to bed and told him to stay there?

Obviously not, a small voice whispered inside her head as she continued staring at a half-naked Travis Cayou. He still had his jeans on, what was left of them, but his shirt was gone, and so were his boots and his socks.

He picked a glass up off the counter, swished it around under the tap, and filled it with cold water for a long drink. She watched his head tilt back and feather an arc of sandy brown hair across the nape of his neck. She watched the way the muscles tightened in his arm and across the top of his body above a torso-wrapping bandage. Tan lines bisected the hard curves of his biceps on both arms, and another tan line ended just below his throat, delineating a sleekly muscled chest. He wiped his mouth with the back of his hand when he was finished, and she found herself following every movement, cocking her head to keep him in view through the window.

Most people looked vulnerable without their clothes on, without their shield against the elements and prying eyes. He did not. Even with his body criss-crossed by bandages, he looked perfectly in charge of his environment, firmly in control, more in control than she felt.

She stood in the softly falling snow, watching him search for something else in the kitchen, knowing she had to get going. She had cows birthing tonight. Curran, her other ranch hand, had to be wondering where she was—and he'd think she'd gone crazy if he knew.

She worked with men, all kinds of men. The ranches were crawling with them. So what was it about Travis Cayou that caused her insides to short-circuit?

His smile . . . Her mouth tightened at that silent truth. She didn't like being intimidated, or being caught off guard. His smile had done both to her, every time. The intimidation was subtle, unnerving on a level she wasn't used to confronting. His smile made her feel out of her depth. It made her feel her inexperience with men, especially men like Travis Cayou. She was one of the best ranch hands in Colorado or Wyoming, but she couldn't flirt her way out of a paper bag.

At least he probably wouldn't be staying long. The thought caused the tightness to ease from her mouth. He'd probably only come home because he'd gotten hurt. There certainly hadn't been any plans for him to come home. The phone call had surprised Shoat right out of his boots.

She could live with her new figuring. He'd be gone before spring roundup. Of course he would. Maybe even sooner, when James got home. She didn't think Travis would stick around very long with James making his life miserable, one of the older Cayou's particular talents when he didn't take to a person.

Fortified, and praying her voice didn't break and her eyes didn't wander, she walked across the porch and opened the kitchen door. The wind picked up just then, blowing her inside with a gust of snow.

Travis shivered and turned toward the opening door. A soft curse slipped out from between his teeth. Her timing was remarkable, as if her one goal in life was to see him at his worst and weakest. His skin was jumping and his nerves were twitching from one end of his body to the other. All he'd wanted was a bottle of whiskey to knock himself out with, and all he'd found was apple juice and water. He couldn't even reach high enough to get himself a coffee cup. Shoat's coffee had been known to pack a punch or two.

"I brought you these," she said, shutting the door and taking a couple of steps inside. She held a small brown plastic bottle out to him.

Travis nearly fell to his one good knee in gratitude. "Thanks," he said softly, trying not to sound over-anxious.

He took the bottle, twisted off the cap, and shook out one pill. Two had knocked him on his butt, and he'd just as soon not need her to carry him up to bed. However tantalizing the opportunities might be, he'd decided earlier he had too much at stake to risk fooling around with one of the ranch hands. Not that Callie looked at all inclined to allow any fooling around, and—he gave her a quick, assessing glance—she sure didn't look like any ranch hand he'd ever worked with. She was prettier than most rodeo queens he'd known, prettier than most women he'd known, in a dark, wild way, with her untamed hair, luminous eyes, and sun-kissed skin.

"I couldn't remember where I'd left them," he continued, concentrating on screwing on the bottle cap, his voice huskier than normal. "I guess I left them with you."

"Sort of," she said. "I thought you might be needing them."

His short burst of laughter was filled with understatement.

"I'm sorry," she said. "I should have—"

"Don't worry about it," he interrupted. "I've lived through worse." His gaze took in her attire, then met her eyes. "Going to a party?"

Her smile was quick, unpremeditated. "Sure. Me and a bunch of two-year-old heifers."

"That's a pretty rough crowd," he said when he found his voice. Her smile had taken his breath away for a moment, or maybe it was just the painkiller kicking in.

His money was on the smile, the flash of white teeth, the teasing curve of her lips, the surprising dimple that creased her cheek close to her mouth. He'd never had any dose of medication punch him in the solar plexus in quite the same way.

"Yeah, well," she said, "they do need a lot of hand-holding."

He grinned. "I must have been doing it all wrong then, 'cause I seem to remember always holding on to the other end."

She laughed and turned to leave, but at the door swung back around. "Would you tell Shoat I might be needing him later? Pete Rankin is running a fever and looking a little green. I should be okay, but if two of them decide to go at once and there's trouble, I'll call him on the walkie-talkie."

"Sure." Travis nodded.

He waited until she'd shut the door, then he limped over to look out the window. A bay horse stood in a circle of light from the yard lamp, blowing clouds of steam and shifting his weight. Snow fell from the dark sky and blew off the porch roof, swirling around the bundled figure swinging herself up into the saddle.

Travis watched until she was only another shadow among the softly rising hills. He'd done his share of riding on cold and thankless nights, but he'd never thought he'd see the day when the CLC sent a woman out alone.

Logically, he knew she was safer out there with the cows than just about anyplace else on God's green earth. Most criminal types didn't even know where Wyoming was, let alone this parcel of Colorado tucked in between the border and the mountains; and cattle rustlers weren't inclined to snatch calving heifers, especially in a snow squall. There might be a mountain lion, but a newborn calf would be an easier dinner than a woman on a horse.

He stood there a while longer, thinking about Callie and wondering why his logic wasn't completely reassuring. It must have something to do with her being so female. He'd known a few women ranch hands and ranch wives who worked out, and he'd be the last person to say they weren't womanly.

Callie was different, though. He wasn't sure how, not yet. It certainly wasn't anything on the surface. Her style was plain, but on her, plain took on a whole new meaning. It meant simply beautiful, without artifice. Her personality was straightforward, too, but there were mysteries galore in her eyes and in what little she said. His instincts kept telling him that her femaleness was affecting his thinking, riling up his natural inclinations, working on everything male in him, but he thought he'd outgrown slavery to his hormones a long time ago.

No, he wasn't at all sure what it was about her, but he had an idea that just thinking about her could keep him up at night.

Callie wrapped her hands around the hot mug of coffee. She needed both the warmth and the sustenance. The snow had stopped just after midnight, and the temperature was dropping, heading for its predawn low. So far the night had been her easiest of the season. She'd had one reluctant momma, but she'd managed to get cow and calf together.

"Are you going to be my trouble spot?" she asked the heifer bedded down in front of her, using a soft voice and soothing tone to counteract the cow's heavy panting.

She took a last sip of coffee and set the cup aside on the hay bale she'd been using as a resting spot. She'd waited long enough for this cow. It was time to find out what was happening in there.

Ten minutes later she called Shoat. She couldn't pull what she couldn't get hold of, and one of the calf's front hooves was just out of her reach no matter how far she leaned in. The heifer's panting had gone from heavy to frantic, interspersed with a few bellows they had to be hearing down at the ranch house.

The voice on the other walkie-talkie wasn't Shoat's, though, and the short "I'll be right up" she got for an answer didn't leave her with a clue. Curran sometimes took over for Shoat, especially if the older man's arthritis was acting up. Pete Rankin might have come around. Jim Kyle might have sent her help from Reese, or James might have come home early.

Travis's coming up never occurred to her, until a tall man eased himself out of the saddle and limped inside the calving shed.

"What's the problem?" he asked, heading straight for the bellowing cow.

"Calf's got a front leg caught back," she managed to say, a little stunned and a whole lot curious about his presence. "I can't quite get a hold of it."

He nodded and shrugged his good arm out of the flannel-lined denim coat. The rest of the coat slid off his other shoulder, revealing his sling and cast. He dropped the coat on a hay bale and, without asking for directions, walked over to the medicine chest and pulled down the bottle of disinfectant.

"Guess I better take a look," he said. "Can you help me with my sleeve?" His eyes met hers across the calving shed.

Now she was a lot stunned. She hesitated, not knowing if she wanted him working on her cows or not. He was a rodeo rider, wasn't he? Not an experienced cow and calf man. He wasn't Shoat.

But she could tell by the way he stood there with the bottle that he was serious—and he was the boss, whether he'd hired her or not.

Wiping her hand on her coveralls, she approached him carefully. "How are you feeling?" she asked, which was as close as she could get to saying "Do you have any idea what you're doing?"

"Fine," he said, catching her eye again and smiling. "If you'll just roll it up for me . . ." His voice trailed off, further explanation unnecessary.

Once again she hesitated, standing in front of him,

staring at his arm. A painful bellow from the heifer startled her into action. She grabbed both sides of his shirtsleeve and started rolling, and when she couldn't roll any more, she pushed, until his arm was bare and her hands were brushing his tight muscles. His skin was warm to her icy fingers, wonderfully warm, but she didn't linger. She didn't dare.

She snatched her hands back when she was finished, deliberately not meeting his eyes, and grabbed the tub of petroleum jelly.

She knelt down beside him when he went to work. It was the sensible thing to do, what she got paid for doing. Either he or the cow or the calf was bound to need her help before the birth was finished. She'd never seen a man with only one good arm pull out a calf.

Of course, she'd noticed that his one good arm was real good, all the muscles in the right places, moving in the right way, all tensile strength and corded power, an arm of steel to hold a Brahma bull or a bronc.

"Come on, momma. Take it easy," she crooned to the heifer, trying to get her mind back on her business.

Fifteen minutes later Travis Cayou had risen a couple of dozen notches on her scale. If she could have hired him, she would have made the offer on the spot. The man was wasted on rodeo shows.

"Nice job," she said, rubbing the calf with a gunny sack, a pleased grin spreading across her face. "Real nice job. Come on, honey. Let's go see your momma." She moved the calf up to its mother's nose and watched the heifer nudge her new baby.

When the calf was nursing, she turned back to Travis. He was standing by the coal-burning stove, doing a poor job of washing off his arm in a bucket of water.

The jeans he was wearing were held up by a tightly cinched leather belt. The telltale ring of a chewing tobacco can was imprinted on one of the faded and patched rear pockets, and the jeans were too short—all signs of a different owner. She didn't have to wonder too long who the jeans belonged to; the patches and the ring told her they belonged to Shoat. He went through more back pockets than a kid, and his jeans were large enough for Travis's bandaged knee to fit inside the leg, even if the younger man's waist was far too narrow to do Shoat's girth justice.

Her first instinct was to help him with his washing up. The cast made the job nothing but a struggle, and he'd done plenty to help her. But he was also standing there in the harsh light cast by the bare bulb above him, looking intently capable, all masculine angles and hard curves.

Despite the frigid chill in the air, his hairline was darkened with dampness, attesting to the energy he'd expended doing her job for her, and still she didn't move for him—until he winced in pain and the washcloth fell from his stiff fingers.

"Callie?" he asked, his voice softly hoarse. "Could you give me a hand?" He turned toward her, lifting his shadowed gaze to meet hers.

She nodded in answer, suddenly not trusting herself to speak. She'd spent more nights than she could count working with one ranch hand or another, but she'd never felt alone with any of them the way she felt alone with Travis. She'd never felt the cold and the darkness form an almost tangible barrier at the shed door, as if the rest of the world had ceased existing.

He was too good-looking by half. But John Torrance, owner of the Torrance Ranch, was good-looking, and he'd even come around to see her a couple of times. He never made her breath catch, or her throat get all tight.

Pulling calves had to be the least romantic thing she could think of, yet with each step she took closer to him, her pulse speeded up in a way she couldn't deny or blame on anything except his dark eyes and the sun-streaked swath of hair swept back off his face. His sideburns were short and darker than the rest of his hair, but not as dark as the deep, rich brown of his eyes. Their color reminded her of the earth at its most promising, soft and welcoming in the spring.

She broke their visual contact when to look any longer would have been too revealing, too painful, and too wonderful all at the same time. Something strange was happening to her, and it had started hours ago, in the Laramie bus station.

She picked up the washcloth, a rag actually, and soaped it thoroughly, all the while wishing she could think of something, anything, to say. But she couldn't get two words to stick together coherently in her mind. He was too quiet, his soft breathing filling the air around her. The only other thing she heard was the pounding of her heart, which tied her tongue into worse knots.

She started at the top of his arm, next to the tight rolls of shirtsleeve, sluicing the water and the suds down to his wrist. She tried to keep the cloth between her hand and his skin, and she absolutely did not lift her gaze past the job needing to be done—though she could see the rise and fall of his chest, and the shift of his hips as he changed position, moving closer to the bucket and her. A sudden need to exhale warned her she was holding her breath.

"Are you okay?" he asked, his voice deep and warm and close, very close.

"Yes," she said, after taking in a much needed breath of air.

"I'll stay the night, if you like."

The words sank in and found a private, unforeseen hope deep in her heart. Her own thoughts shocked her as heat raced across her skin like wildfire. She dropped the soapy rag on the concrete slab holding the old stove and almost tipped the bucket over in her haste to retrieve it.

Travis caught the bucket with his good hand and lightly touched her arm with the back of the fingers of the other hand. "Are you sure you're okay?"

She nodded and squeezed the rag out in the bucket. He would have teased her, something about the cat getting her tongue, but she looked too fragile, and he didn't trust himself even to look at her much longer, let alone start any kind of teasing.

Because she was a tease just by being there. Midnight curls had escaped her braid and danced in tantalizing circlets around her face, asking for a helping touch. Her downcast eyes layered a thick feathering of lashes against her tawny cheeks. Her too-sweet mouth was slightly parted, naively seductive, waiting only for the warmth of his kiss.

"Callie?"

She looked up, innocently giving him the access he wanted. He brushed her cheek with the backs of his fingers, careful not to let his cast graze her skin. She was so pretty.

Holding her with the barest of pressure, he lowered his mouth to hers. His lips caressed hers, gently, tentatively, once, then twice, and he felt her sigh. She softened toward him, leaning without moving. He kissed her again, a brief touch, rubbing his mouth across hers and back again, then once more, and this time her movement was perceptible.

He lifted his head to see her face, and what he saw sent a heavy wave of heat through his veins. Her eyes were dark with unspoken need, unexpected pleasure. Groaning softly, he covered her mouth with his own, demanding she give what they both wanted. He stroked his thumb up her cheek and tasted her lips with his tongue, asking and asking, until her mouth opened and he slipped inside to a little piece of heaven.

Callie moaned helplessly, clinging to him, completely overwhelmed by the sensations ricocheting through her. He was hot, so very hot, his body a hard wall of strength against her melting acquiescence. His tongue probed, and she felt a quickening in her womb. His fingers tunneled into her hair, and her hands slid across his shoulders, holding him closer, wanting to touch him and feel his muscles tighten in response.

She returned his kiss as if she'd never let him go, and Travis knew it. He didn't want to stop either, but to go on and on, until she was his, until he'd tasted her sweetness and she'd eased the fire building in his core.

That wasn't going to happen, though, not tonight. Years ago he might have kept pushing, especially given her response. He'd certainly made love when he'd been busted up worse than he was right then. But he wasn't a boy anymore, and Callie wasn't one of the girls he used to know.

Shoat had explained she was the foreman, a damn good one, and Travis didn't see himself getting anywhere but into trouble by seducing the foreman.

Yet in his arms she didn't feel like the boss. She didn't feel like any woman he'd ever known, and that was enough to make him back off.

He angled his next kiss to the corner of her lips, then slid his mouth up her cheek. He kissed the side of his nose and her closed eyes. He kissed both temples, softly, with a sigh, and her brow, and it took everything he had not to start all over again. With his hand under her arm, he felt the rise of her breasts with every breath she took. He felt her willingness, and her need, and he felt the hesitation underlying it all.

He pulled her close and tucked her head under his chin, holding her until her breaths were smooth and easy, until his own reaction had mellowed to a manageable level. Even then he didn't want to let her go.

Callie rested against his chest, her eyes squeezed shut in mortification. She didn't believe what she'd let happen. She didn't believe how badly she wanted it to happen again. Hadn't she learned anything about life? About who got what in this world and why? Hadn't she decided the cost of heartache was too high a price to pay for any man's love?

Who was Travis Cayou to mess up her plans? What kind of fool had she become in the last twelve hours?

"I've got to check the cows," she said bluntly, pushing away.

She didn't look at him. She stalked out of the calving shed and swung herself up on the bay horse, and if she had to wipe tears off her face on the ride through the pasture, she made damn sure he didn't see her do it.

Four

Travis spent the rest of the night in the calving shed, stoking the stove to keep the coffee warm, putting the heifers she brought in into stalls, checking the new calves. More than once she found him stretched out on a couple of hay bales, or sitting propped against the wall, half asleep next to the stove. Any other cowboy would have gotten the bottom of his boots kicked for dozing on the job, but she let Travis be, amazed he was able to keep going at all.

Truth be told, she preferred him at less than full strength. She had a hard enough time facing him after that kiss without having to talk to him every time she drove in a cow. Fortunately, the rest of the night went smoothly, and he didn't need a lot of direction when it came to cows and calves. He just did the job, and next to Shoat he was the best she'd seen. The old man had found an apt pupil in the younger Cayou.

Dawn finally came, and with it Shoat, mustache bristling with frost by the time he rode up to the calving sheds. Not far behind him was Pete Rankin, slumped over in his saddle but coming to work nonetheless. Callie gave herself a pat on the back for reading him right.

Travis had fallen asleep again about a half hour earlier, and after talking with Shoat, she took the coward's way out and rode home alone. He'd either wake up on his own or Shoat would take care of him. He wasn't her responsibility, or her boss, really. She didn't know what he was—except the most incredibly seductive man she'd ever kissed.

She inhaled a deep breath and let it out on a heavy sigh. She'd been crazy to kiss him like that. But she'd never tasted anything as erotically compelling as his mouth. He'd touched her, and she'd wanted more. The sensations he'd started with the first teasing caress of his lips had exploded down her nervous system like fires, igniting emotions she'd thought extinct. For the first time in her life, she thought she understood why some women became such fools. It was a lesson she would have preferred not learning.

It had taken her own mother years to learn it. Some of Callie's earliest memories were of moving in the middle of the night, of being kicked out when one of her mother's love affairs went bad. Over the years, though, the boyfriends had become fewer and further apart, and older and less wild. There hadn't been as many cowboys and no rodeo riders. Through most of her teenage years there hadn't been anyone at all. By the time Callie was eighteen and ready to leave, her mother had settled into a home and a job in Cheyenne. Recently, she'd begun dating an accountant, and they were thinking of marrying in the summer.

Remembering her mother's pain and the insecurity she herself had suffered, Callie stiffened her determination to avoid Travis. He couldn't just show up out of nowhere and turn her insides upside down, she told herself. She wouldn't allow it. She wasn't naive. She knew the facts of life. This chemistry thing, or initial attraction, or whatever, was purely ridiculous, adolescent. It didn't have anything to do with real life. It didn't have anything to do with Callie Michael and what she wanted.

The main house came into view beneath the slope of a rise, and she tucked her scarf tighter around the opening of her coat. Her life was here, on the home ranch of the Cayou Land and Cattle Company, and nothing could ruin it faster for her than to tangle herself up with one of the Cayous.

Curran was in the barn, feeding the horses and milking the cows when she arrived. An older man, though younger than Shoat, Curran had a lean and weathered face, with deep lines fanning out from the corners of his pale blue eyes. Tufts of salt and pepper hair stuck out on either side of his battered cowboy hat. She nodded a greeting to him, then carried the milk up to the house. Curran would load the sled with hay while she ate. Only after the cows were fed would she enjoy the luxury of a hot shower and sleep.

As she pulled a plate of pancakes from the oven, she tried to understand once more why James had chosen such a poor time to be away from the ranch. All his talk about "ripe deals" had sounded like excuses to her. He was her boss and he had her loyalty, but she often wished he'd either give her the control she needed to run the ranch correctly, or help more himself. Half of one and half of the other made her job more difficult than necessary.

She poured hot syrup over her stack of pancakes and sat down to take her first bite. Her fork barely got off the plate when the door opened behind her. She knew without looking who it was, because every muscle she had tensed in a way she'd been fighting all night long. She slowly lowered her fork back to the plate, wishing she'd skipped breakfast.

"Mornin'." His voice was gravelly with sleep and tiredness. It's huskiness reverberated across her senses like an overload of electricity, leaving her hyperaware of his presence and nervous as a cat.

Staring at her plate, she took a steadying breath and said, "Breakfast is in the oven. Shoat left plenty."

A few seconds later she heard the squeak of the oven door.

Travis peaked inside at the pile of pancakes and bacon and wondered if he had the strength to eat. He compromised by putting as little effort into the process as possible, wrapping a few pieces of bacon inside one of Shoat's oversized pancakes and eating it like a burrito. No butter, no syrup, no wasted energy. He wanted to save what little energy he had for a more important matter—an apology, the likes of which he'd never thought he'd have to make again.

"I'm sorry about last night. I didn't mean for anything like that to happen," he said, standing behind her and watching her push her pancakes around on her plate. She looked as worn-out as he felt. Smudges of weariness blued the skin beneath her eyes. Her hair was more mess than braid, and her hands were red and chapped from the cold.

He remembered how little any of that had mattered when he'd whispered her name and she'd melted like hot honey in his arms, her mouth soft and sweet and hungry on his, the fire they'd lit between them drugging in its intensity. For a moment, when she'd clung to him, her breasts crushed against his chest, her thighs pressed against his, he'd forgotten his pain and the cold. He'd forgotten she was the foreman.

He wouldn't forget again. Coming home was complicated enough.

"You don't have to worry about it happening again," he continued, telling himself as well as her. She'd stopped pushing pancakes and was tapping her fork. She'd pushed back slightly from the table, too, the toes of her boots pressed into the floor, her heels lifted.

She was going to bolt. He knew it, and a part of him rebelled. He didn't want her running away. If he was going to stay, and he was, they needed to be partners, not adversaries.

"Good," she said, and made her move.

He was faster, wrapping his hand around her arm as she stood and turned to leave. Her eyes flashed up to his and held, despite the color infusing her cheeks.

He waited, watching her blush spread as her breaths grew shallow. She didn't pull away from him. She just stood there, gazing at him with a challenge in her eyes, a challenge he couldn't resist.

"You could have always said no, Callie." He spoke quietly, his voice soft and intense.

Her blush deepened, but she still held her ground, and suddenly all his good intentions were for naught. He was so close to kissing her again he could almost feel the warmth of her lips and taste the memory of her mouth on his tongue.

Of its own accord, his thumb stroked across her arm, then his fingers applied a gentle pressure, guiding her closer. He'd never considered himself the imaginative type, but the darkening, softening depths of her eyes were making his thoughts run wild, taking him beyond a kiss to the sweet warmth promised by her body as it came nearer.

He swore under his breath and tightened his one-handed hold on her. What was happening to him was happening fast and had all the signs of a major erotic disaster. If he'd been with anyone except Callie, he might have laughed, considering the rest of his physical condition. If his arousal had been any less intense, he might have backed away again.

But when he looked at her, all he wondered was how he'd backed off the first time. She was no less enticing for being tired. If anything, her weariness made her more approachable, more vulnerable, more welcoming of his strength to lean upon.

He had an irresistible need to seal his mouth over hers, to glide his tongue down the length of hers, to mate with her in any way possible, to claim her, this dark-haired beauty. The need was sexual. It was real. He didn't even attempt to hide his intentions. He wanted her to know what this kiss meant, what it was, and to know what allowing it meant to him.

Callie knew. Her heart pounded with the knowledge, and the remnants of her common sense warned her to get out now, before it was too late, before he touched her again and gave her yet one more taste of his magic. Travis Cayou was no good, and no good for her. Any fool could see it.

But any fool wasn't standing there close enough to feel his need, to feel the dark warmth of his eyes draw her in, to feel something as intrinsically male as his body pressed close to hers, reminding her she was pure female on the inside.

She wanted him. She wanted to be taken by him. The truth was shocking, but inescapable. When he pulled her one step closer, so that every breath he took demanded a breath from her, she knew she was lost.

He acknowledged her acceptance of the inevitable with the briefest smile, which in no way lessened the intensity of his gaze. She didn't know if she detected victory or relief in the slight gesture, but neither mattered as his mouth came down on hers.

Her eyes drifted closed, and with the first stroke of his tongue across her lips, she melted in slow waves from the inside out. Sweet longing met insistent need in his arms, binding her to him in a spiral of growing desire. Her mouth parted, welcoming his pantomime of lovemaking. Her fingers threaded through the hair brushing the back of his collar, and she felt the muscles in his arm flex and tighten around her.

His rough breathing echoed in her ear, adding fuel to the fire fanning to life way down inside her. She moved against him.

Travis groaned in pleasure and spread his legs to fit her more closely to him. He slanted his mouth across hers, deepening the kiss, drawing her ever nearer. He needed two good arms to do what he wanted, to lift her and carry her up to his room, where with any luck at all, he'd make love to her for the rest of the day. Once wouldn't be enough, never enough.

He opened his mouth wider over hers, feeling his frustration grow with his arousal. She was giving everything with her kiss, but it was no more than a kiss. The same hesitation he'd felt in her before was telling him he wasn't going to get more than a kiss, not from Callie Michael, not this morning. There were ways, though, of turning a kiss into something more.

He slipped his hand up to her breast and captured

her gasp with his mouth. Lord, she felt good. Soft and fuller than he'd expected, and willing, if he believed the subtle way she filled his palm. He let his hand drift back down to her waist and began tugging at her shirt, all the while cursing the bull that had broken his other wrist.

The slamming of the door stopped him in mid-tug. For an eternal second, her mouth stilled under his. Then she was away from him, leaving him too stunned to react quickly enough to hold on to her. He forced his gaze from her to the intruder and swore softly.

"'Scuse me, Travis, Callie." Shoat dragged his hat off his balding head, looking sheepish, though a small smile played around his mouth. "Thought you'd both be finishing up by now. 'Specially you, Travis. Didn't look to me like you had an ounce of energy to spare when you left the sheds this morning. Never figured you'd be—"

"Shoat," Travis warned.

"Well, boy. It's the truth." Shoat was outright grinning and chuckling now. "I only came back to the house to make sure you hadn't fallen off your horse into the snow somewheres where we wouldn't find you until the end of the week or something. Never occurred to me you was quite so motivated to make it to the kitchen, and I ain't talking about my cooking neither." He slapped his hat across his knee and let out a good laugh.

Callie had heard enough. She knew where the front door was, and she didn't hesitate to use it. She turned on her heels and stalked out of the kitchen.

"Callie."

She heard Travis call her name, but she kept on walking, fast and sure of her destination, which was anywhere far enough away from him for her to regain her sanity.

Callie's last heifer calved out the third week in April. She'd managed to avoid Travis completely for the first couple of days he was home. One night working in the snow and cold had put him in bed for the next two, with Shoat fussing and worrying over him like a mother hen.

She hadn't been able to avoid him that weekend, when he'd insisted on being up and around, so she'd ignored him instead, using her greater mobility and many responsibilities to duck out of conversations and greetings. By the middle of the second week, she'd lost most of her edge in the mobility department, and Shoat had started to interfere with her responsibilities, rearranging her priorities for her.

"Somebody's got to do it," he said one afternoon, "and I ain't up to it, Callie. I just ain't up to it." He bent over to rub his bowlegged knee. "I got pain here, real pain."

Callie didn't know what to believe. The man had been wizened since the day she'd been hired, but he'd never complained, at least not the way he had been lately. And he seemed spry enough whenever he thought her back was turned.

"All's I'm asking," he went on, "is for you to pick up the supplies and do a little shopping. Loretta will have most of the order boxed up, but I need some extras."

"She'll be awful disappointed not to see you," Callie said, scraping her plate off into the sink. Lunch had been one of Shoat's less successful efforts to date. If nothing else, she wouldn't mind going into Laramie and finding him a new cookbook. But she and Curran had fences to fix.

"Loretta knows I'm a busy man. She ain't going anywhere."

"She's not getting any younger, either," Callie countered. Shoat and the grocery clerk had been dating for over a year, and despite what he might think, Callie knew Loretta harbored hopes of the marrying kind. "You really ought to go in and see her."

"Nope. I can't. It's my leg, Callie."

She still didn't believe him. "What about Pete? He's coming down from Reese tomorrow. I can make do without him and send him to town for you."

Shoat snorted. "That boy's never been grocery shopping in his life. He wouldn't know a bag of beans from a doughnut hole."

He was probably right, but that wasn't why Callie gave in. She was tired of arguing with Shoat, and she was darn tired of eating his "whatever's left in the pantry" meals.

"Okay. Get your list. I'm going."

"Good. Good." He practically skipped out of the kitchen, leaving Callie with a much-narrowed gaze and a nagging sense of suspicion. What was the old geezer up to? she wondered.

She wondered right up to when she opened the pickup truck door and saw Travis sitting on the passenger side. Anger kept her from being totally embarrassed and gave her enough courage to get in and pretend he was just a passenger, just like any other cowboy who needed a ride into town now and then.

Shoat had set her up for reasons she didn't want to acknowledge. He had to know better than to try to matchmake, but nothing else made sense. She'd have to have a talk with him, remind him she was the ramrod of the outfit.

"Hello, Travis," she said, jamming the truck into gear.

"Hi, Callie. How are you doing?"

"Fine. Just fine," she assured him, then cranked up the radio.

That was all right with Travis. He didn't mind just looking at her. In the past couple of days he'd decided what to do with her, and it didn't include any more apologies or guarantees he couldn't keep. It also didn't include scaring her off again.

He'd been watching her since he'd come home, mostly from a distance but enough to realize a few things about her.

His brother ought to be shot, for one. Travis had never allowed anyone to take advantage of him the way James was taking advantage of Callie. He doubted if there was another ranch in northern Colorado or southern Wyoming that would have given her the opportunities James had, but she was paying for them in hard labor and being reimbursed at about two thirds the going rate in salary. The problem had been easy to fix. A few minutes at the computer had made being foreman of the home ranch of the CLC a nominally better job. No one would ever get rich at it, and Travis would have done the same if she'd been a man doing the job she was doing.

By his reckoning, there were places to save money and places to spend. The cows and the hands weren't a place to skimp. If he'd wanted to save money, he'd found a number of places in the budget, mostly those concerned with James's personal accounts. His brother needed to be reined in. Travis wasn't looking forward to doing it, but he'd be damned if he let James suck the ranch dry.

Shoat was right. He'd been gone too long. The CLC was coasting, and good ranches didn't stay good ranches very long by coasting without a strong hand at the helm. Good as she was, Callie couldn't be that hand, and James wasn't acting like a man who wanted the job.

Travis wanted the job, and every day of the last week and a half he'd been taking it, piece by piece. Between him and Callie, there wouldn't be anything left for James if he ever decided to come home.

He and Callie. They were starting to make quite a team, whether she knew it or not. He knew she had a stubborn streak, but a man didn't get to be a champion bronc rider without learning a few ways to deal with stubborn.

She also had a self-defense mechanism set on instant automatic, and he didn't know why. Not even Shoat had been able to help him in that department. All Shoat knew was that she'd shown up three years earlier, highly recommended, and had dug in and gotten the job done.

She also had a kiss that made a man forget everything else.

He leaned forward and turned the radio down.

"I went over to see Jim Kyle at Reese yesterday. He said to tell you thanks for sending him Pete. The boy is working out fine. He says you've got a real knack for hiring." Business, Travis had decided, was the safest form of conversation for her, and he wanted her to get used to him being involved in the business of the ranch.

"I'm careful, that's all," she said, but he saw a blush of pleasure bloom on her cheek.

"He's worried about this grazing fee thing in Washington. I told him I'd talk to you to see what we'd done."

Her blush deepened, and he knew it wasn't in pleasure.

"James talked to Congressman Sealy a couple of months ago, just before he left for the East Coast," she said. She paused, her eyes fixed straight ahead on the road, then added, "But he didn't get anywhere with him. Last I heard, he was voting against us."

"Didn't James call him again?"

"He tried. The congressman stopped taking his calls. I think James planned on talking with a lobbyist in Washington or something like that. All I know is that somebody better tell the government we can't pay four times as much for graze and still make a living out here. It's crazy."

"Guess I better call Bob Sealy, then."

She eyed him warily. "You're sure welcome to give it a try, but like I said, James didn't have much luck."

"I'm not James," he said, reaching in his shirt pocket and pulling out a small notebook.

So I noticed, Callie thought, wondering what was in the notebook he was flipping through. She didn't have to wait long to find out.

"I talked to Everett up at Connor's Place," he said, referring to the third foreman of the CLC. "He's going to get back to me by Monday with his hardware needs, including fencing. So is Jim Kyle. If you can tell me what you need, I'll arrange for one big buy. We'll get a better discount, and next year we'll coordinate from the beginning and try to buy direct from the manufacturer. We're a big outfit. We need to start acting like one again."

Callie couldn't have agreed more, but his announcement sent a ripple of uneasiness through her. He was taking over, and sounding damned confident about his ability and his right to do so. She didn't know where that left her, except out in the cold. If James had taken even a tenth more interest in the doings of the CLC, she wouldn't have been needed.

His brother seemed a lot more interested than a tenth. Inside of five minutes, he'd committed to two of her high-priority items. It was going to be real interesting to see if he could put pressure on the congressman and come up with a workable system for bulk buying between all three ranches. Bob Sealy didn't seem interested in talking to any ranchers right now, and the three ranches of the CLC had been going their own way since before she'd come on board.

"James likes things set up the way they are," she said out of loyalty to the man who'd given her a chance.

"James isn't here." He didn't even bother to glance up from his notebook, and Callie let his statement ride. He was right.

She couldn't help him at all with the congressman, but she would help him with the buying as best she could. She only hoped she wasn't helping herself out of a job. Between the three ranches, she was the newest and the most expendable manager. But she guessed Travis had already figured that out.

James called later that night. Travis was gone, spending a few days working Reese, the biggest operation of the CLC. Shoat was already asleep, and Curran never answered the phone, claiming it was never for him and he didn't like disappointing people.

Callie didn't like disappointing people either, especially people who signed her paycheck. So she talked to James about calving season and weather losses, about the price of beef and shipping costs. She talked about firing Bill Webster and about the new hand she'd put on the payroll. She gave him the rundown on Reese and Connor's, according to Jim Kyle's and Everett Shaw's reports. She told him everything was going along fine and that it looked to be a wet year.

She was going to tell him about Travis, right at the end. She'd debated with herself throughout the whole conversation, finally deciding she owed it to James to let him know. She waited too long, though, because before she could even form Travis's name, James was saying he had to go and hung up. Callie hung up, too, wondering if she'd just made a mistake.

Five

A month later Callie knew her uneasiness over Travis's plans fell far short of the mark. Downright fear would have been more appropriate. The man was taking over, and there wasn't a sign of anyone on the horizon able to stop him, least of all James.

James. She shifted uneasily in her breakfast chair, more than aware of the salary increase in the paycheck that had been waiting for her on the table that morning. If James had authorized it, he sure hadn't mentioned it on the phone the other night. And if he hadn't authorized it, what was she supposed to do?

What was Travis up to? she wondered, feeling the ground growing ever less stable under her feet. Regardless, she had a ranch to run. At least she thought she did.

"Somebody has to get to work on the tractor," she said to Shoat. She reached across the table and lifted the coffeepot off its hot plate to pour herself a refill. "When Pete hired on, he said he was a mechanic. Call Reese Park and see if we can get him back here for a few days. Promise them a cake or something. You're always good for an irresistible bribe."

"Don't need to," Shoat said around a mouthful of toast.

"What?" Callie asked, hoping she hadn't heard him right.

"Travis—" Shoat started, but didn't get a chance to finish.

"Dammit!" Callie dropped the old enamel coffeepot on the table, spilling hot coffee all over her cup and saucer, even into her scrambled eggs. "Dammit all!"

Short grabbed the hot pad and moved the pot back onto it, before it burned too large a hole in the tablecloth.

"Dammit!" Callie swore again, pouring the coffee off her eggs and toast and onto the empty serving platter. All it took was the mention of his name to set her off. She was good at her job, damn good. But she couldn't think, and manage, and decide things fast enough to keep up with him, let alone get ahead of him.

Where in the hell did he find the time? she wondered. It wasn't just the home ranch he was taking over. He spent half the week at Reese and a day or more at Connor's. She hadn't heard any complaints from the cow crews or from Jim or Everett, but maybe he wasn't taking over so much with them.

"When?" she snapped, knowing Shoat understood what she was asking. Too many of their conversations ended up the same way lately.

"While you and Curran moved the south herd over on to that new patch of BLM land yesterday. The boy always was good with his hands." As usual, Shoat wasn't the least upset about an occurrence that had her biting bullets, and as usual, whenever he mentioned Travis he puffed up with a bit of pride.

The first couple of times Travis had interfered with her schedule, and her schedule for Curran, he'd saved her so much time, so much work, she'd gathered up all her courage to graciously thank him. But he didn't know when to quit. It was time somebody told him.

She gave her ruined breakfast one last discouraged look before pushing away from the table. Reaching the back door, she jammed her hat on and shrugged into a short denim jacket that was missing both elbows. The collar was a frayed remnant of its original blue corduroy.

"Where is he?" she asked, shoving her gloves into one of the jacket pockets.

"The barn."

She let herself out, and if she heard Shoat whistling a tune before the screen door slammed shut, she wasn't about to mention it.

Her boots sounded a steady rhythm across the back porch and down the steps, fortifying her resolve to get a few things straight with Mr. Travis Cayou. If he wanted her job, he could probably have it without so much as a by-your-leave. She didn't have a contract. She maintained her position purely on the basis of her work and her results. But if he didn't want her job, he had to back off and give her more breathing room. She didn't know which was worse, James dumping the whole ranch on her, or Travis whipping it out from under her feet.

At least he hadn't kissed her since the disaster Shoat had witnessed in the kitchen, and she ought to be thankful. She didn't want to admit even to herself why she wasn't.

She remembered a time not so long ago, when thinking about a sickly cow was the most likely thing to keep her awake at night. Things had changed with his kiss. The memory of the taste of him, the feel of him, had taken precedence over anything a cow might come up with to get her attention.

The dreams were the worst—or the best, depending on her point of view. She could allow herself to luxuriate in the sensual mysteries her mind conjured up, or she could try to douse them with cold rationality. Either way, he was there, all the way down in her subconscious, sneaking up on her in her dreams to entice and thrill her with his hands caressing her, his mouth kissing her with a slowly torturous skill.

Her steps faltered halfway to the barn as an embarrassingly familiar question forced its way into her mind—Why hadn't he tried to kiss her again?

The question lingered until she gave herself the same worn-out answer she'd been using for weeks to salve her emotions and disguise her longing.

Because he's got twice the sense you do, Callie Michael. She lifted her chin and picked up her pace.

She found him in the tack room. He was standing next to his open rigging bag, lost in thought as he worked a goatskin glove onto his left hand. She knew it was his bronc-and-bull-riding glove. Resin shone on the palm and the fingers, and the leather had taken on the shape of his hand.

He had a strip of leather clenched between his teeth,and for a moment she thought he was going to tie the glove on as he must have done a thousand times, cinching it tight over his taped hand and arm. Every chance he had depended on how well the glove stayed wrapped around his bull rope or his rigging, and how well he stayed in the glove.

She hesitated, watching a slight wince narrow his gaze as he pulled too hard with the fingers of his recently healed wrist. Suddenly she hoped he didn't tie the glove on.

The instant the thought crossed her mind, she knew it was ridiculous and female. He'd been riding bulls the night before he'd dragged himself into the Laramie bus station, and it hadn't been the first time he'd gotten busted up. He'd been a rodeo cowboy long before she'd met him, and he'd probably be one long after their paths parted. But what she hadn't known in that bus station was that he was much more.

If he was footloose, he sure had a funny way of sticking around, even on Saturday nights. If he was the irresponsible member of the family, he ought to be giving lessons to James, whose brand of responsibility had been pushing her to her limit. If he was good for nothing, then nothing had never looked so good.

And if you're not careful, Callie, you're going to get your heart broken. The warning was too late. She knew it just by looking at him.

"Damn," she whispered, turning to leave.

"Callie?" His voice stopped her. "Did you need something?"

Knowing she'd given herself away, she slowly turned back to face him.

"No, not really," she said, her tone short, her hand clenched in irritation at herself. "I just wanted to thank you for tuning up the tractor and getting it ready. I didn't mean to interrupt anything."

Lord, she hated herself for being such a coward.

"You're not interrupting anything except a few memories, and you're welcome on the tractor. That hunk of metal and I go way back." He grinned, deepening the crease in one lean cheek, and her heart did a slow slide into the pit of her stomach.

"Yeah, well, thanks." She needed to get away from him and took a tentative step backward. It didn't do her a whole lot of good, because he took a step forward.

"I was just getting ready to come in to see you. Figured you'd still be at breakfast."

"Oh." She took another step and her boot hit the wall, or the doorjamb. She couldn't tell which and wasn't about to turn around and make a complete fool of herself to find out.

"Bob Sealy is expected back in his office today," he went on. "I'm going to give him a call, see if I can set up an appointment to go down and see him. I wanted to know if you thought I should ask one of the other ranchers to meet with him."

"Oh."

He was still coming toward her, and she was having a hard time concentrating on what he was saying.

"Who's president of the Stockgrowers Association this year?" He stopped in the nick of time to keep her from heading out at a dead run. Leaning his hip against one of the saddles stored in the tack room, he shifted his weight off his bad knee. She'd noticed him doing that many times and had often wondered how much pain he was still in. Typically, she hadn't come right out and asked him.

The thought gave her a pause. She would have asked any of the other cowboys.

"Torrance," she answered him, her tone mellowing with guilt and chagrin. "John Torrance."

"Good man," he said. "He must be putting some kind of pressure on the congressman. It's not like John to let his politicians get away from him."

"He's tried, but ran into the same problem James

did. Sealy stopped taking his calls, and nobody has time to go down there and camp on his doorstep."

"Well, I'm not planning on camping either." He shifted his gaze to the saddle and wrapped his gloved hand around the pommel, testing his grip. "I'd like you to come. I'll need someone to drive, and as the foreman of the home ranch, you're the most logical one to go."

Actually, Travis admitted, logic didn't have a damn thing to do with it. He wanted her to come so he could spend the whole day with her and have an excuse to take her out to dinner.

Keeping everything businesslike between them was an annoying strain, but at least she wasn't running off every time he got near her. Better yet, this morning she'd actually come looking for him again.

He didn't have a real plan for winning her over. He'd been living by the seat of his pants too long to plan anything. But he did have a growing need, and a method in mind for assuaging the ache she gave him whether she was running away or standing her ground. It wasn't a purely physical pain, like the one in his knee or the one in his rib cage, though there was a physical side to the frustration she inspired.

It was the emotional side to it that had taken him by surprise and still confused him. He wanted to be a part of her, of her world, which coincidentally was his. He wanted to know where she'd come from and where she wanted to go. He wanted to know what she thought about in the middle of the night when he was awake thinking about her. He wanted to know if they could start another meltdown by kissing again, and he wanted to know how long he'd have to wait to find out.

"What do you say, Callie? Will you come with me

to see Bob Sealy?" He reflexively tightened his hold on the pommel, waiting for her answer.

"You seem awful sure he's going to see you," she said, not bothering to hide her doubts.

"Oh, he'll see me. Don't worry about that part." He smiled wryly, then glanced up at her. "Will you come?"

"Sure," she said, still doubtful. "There isn't a rancher or a cowhand for a hundred miles who doesn't want a chance at Bob Sealy right now."

"Great." The smile returned to his face, natural and easy, and oh so dangerous to her heart. He held her gaze for a moment, intensifying her peril and causing her to unconsciously deepen her breaths. Then he checked his watch. "Guess I'll go put in my call. I want to be the first thing on his agenda when he hits the state line."

"Travis?" She stopped him when he would have passed her, and that was a mistake. It brought him too close, within touching distance. But her curiosity was greater than the unsettled emotions he always brought to life in her. "What makes you so sure he'll see you?"

He didn't answer right away, just looked at her, fighting a grin. "I did him a favor a few years back, a really big favor," he finally admitted.

"What?" she asked before she had time to talk herself out of prying.

The grin broadened, and he dropped his gaze, chuckling softly. "Hell, Callie. I didn't marry his daughter. The man would probably give me the moon if he could get a kickback on it."

Still chuckling, he lifted his hat and dragged his hand through his hair, then settled the Stetson back low on his head, catching and holding her gaze in the middle of the movement. For an instant she thought he was going to take the final step to her and give her a quick kiss. The action would have been perfectly natural, what with the smile lingering on his mouth and her whole self breathless with anticipation.

But he didn't. He winked instead, his grin broadening before he turned and left. Callie stared after him as he walked down the length of the barn. He'd done it again, whipped the ground right out from under her, with a congressman's daughter of all things.

She'd bet anything the poor little rich girl hadn't liked losing her rodeo cowboy. She could only hope it had all happened so many years ago that nobody cared anymore—nobody except her.

Standing in the lobby of the Federal Building, John Torrance looked every inch the successful rancher, from the fresh polish on his boots to the crown of his new hat—white for the good guys, he'd said. He clapped Travis on the back and gave Callie's shoulders a squeeze.

John's dark hair was swept back off his classically handsome face, and his broad smile revealed even white teeth and a hint of mischief in his blue eyes. But he'd never set her heart to pounding the way Travis did with the slightest glance.

He and Travis had already spent a few evenings on the phone discussing their goals for the meeting and their strategies for meeting those goals. Callie had been privy to a couple of the phone calls, and she'd been suitably impressed with what Travis had said. The man was a natural-born rancher, with a rancher's instincts, a rancher's cares. James never should have run him off.

That's what she was beginning to think must have

happened. All those stories about Travis packing up and trying to run away with James's ex-wife during spring roundup were beginning to tarnish. She didn't have any trouble believing the part about the ex-wife, but she had a damn hard time imagining Travis leaving during roundup. The man she knew would have picked a better time.

"How have you been, Callie?" John asked, lightly slipping his arm back around her shoulders. "I've wanted to get down and see you, but I've been shorthanded this spring. Heard you were having the same problem until Travis here came home." He glanced up at Travis. "Your timing couldn't have been better."

"I've got a bull to thank for that," Travis said. He forced a grin onto his face as he wondered what in the hell was going on between Torrance's arm and Callie's shoulders.

"Well, you'll have to take full credit for setting up this meeting," John said. "Nobody else has been able to get their foot in the door, let alone get in to see him. Thanks."

"You're welcome," Travis said, thinking that if Torrance was really so grateful, the least he could do was to get his hands off Travis's woman.

He caught Callie's gaze to see if he could get a reading on the situation, but the uneasiness he detected in her eyes could have meant any number of things.

John had put his arm around her with the ease of familiarity, as if he were like an older brother to her. Even as he thought that one, Travis had a hard time buying it. Any man who wasn't Callie's brother wasn't likely to settle for brotherly affection.

Maybe—and this was an unpleasant thought— maybe she was practically engaged to John Torrance and felt guilty as hell for kissing him to the point of heavy breathing, wet mouths, and searching hands. She wasn't married, however, and though he'd drawn the line at wedding bands a long time ago, anything short of marriage made a woman fair game in Travis's book. Looking at her and John together, knowing exactly what was going through John's mind even if Callie's feelings remained a mystery, Travis knew he better make his move. The time for playing it safe was over, or he was going to lose out, and he was damn tired of losing.

"I guess we better get up there, before the good congressman hightails it back to Washington," he said, reaching for Callie's elbow and subtly leading her away from Torrance. He'd laid down the gauntlet, and the other man's quickly assessing gaze told him the message had been received.

For all their hours on the phone, the meeting didn't go as planned. Congressman Bob proved slippery as an eel when it came to facts, let alone opinions and leanings and justifications. Those he could twist and mangle at will. The facts he just ignored with a neat little side-step of reality.

"Eight-dollar-a-pound hamburger?" he exclaimed to Travis. "Not in our lifetime, no matter what happens in Congress. The people won't abide by it."

Bob Sealy sat back and loosened his tie. Generous amounts of gray were sprinkled through his trimly cut brown hair. His suit was tailored to perfection, dark blue and crisp, but the representative himself looked weary.

"Four times the cost to produce means four times the price," Travis said evenly, forgoing all his numbers and charts and computer-generated fact sheets, and putting it as simply as possible in hopes of finally getting his point across.

"Not necessarily," the congressman begged to differ, as he'd been begging all afternoon. "There are other factors figured in along the way. Factors outside the individual rancher's control."

Travis gave up on tact.

"Maybe you can slip and slide around it on paper, and maybe you can whitewash it to the voters by painting yourself 'environmental green', but the bottom line is you're going to wipe out a whole bunch of those individual ranchers if you vote for an increase of this magnitude, and you *will* see a substantial rise in the price of beef." He leaned forward and picked up a sheaf of papers from the congressman's desk. "You ought to come out and take a look at the Cayou Land and Cattle Company, the biggest ranch in your district. Let me take you out and show you the rangeland you're so committed to protecting from grazing. I guarantee you it's in better than *fair* condition."

Much of the problem with the grazing fee controversy revolved around the ambiguity of the word "fair" to describe the condition of the federal rangelands leased to ranchers.

"A lot of my constituents think the ranchers have been getting a free ride at the taxpayer's expense," the congressman said.

"A lot of people think a lot of things, especially in Washington," Travis countered. "The people of Colorado are paying you to think for yourself."

Callie noticed the slight color rising in Bob Sealy's cheeks and hazarded a quick glance at Travis. His tone had been congenial, but his expression was pure dare.

"The Stockgrowers Association threw a lot of weight behind you last year," John said, stepping in with the second volley. "We'll fight you all the way if you let the grazing fee hike go into effect."

"Gentlemen." Bob Sealy pushed away from his desk and stood up. "I've supported the ranchers for most of my life, but the time has passed when the cattle barons ran this part of the country, and a man, especially a representative of the people, has to consider—"

The buzzing of his telephone interrupted the congressional speech. Nodding apologetically to his three visitors, he lifted the receiver and listened for a moment. True distress flooded his face. His gaze shifted to the door of his office and froze there, as if the sheer weight of his will could keep it closed.

"No," he said softly, intently. "Absolutely not. I'm in a meeting. Tell her to go away, I mean to come back later, to–"

It was too late. The door swung open, and a woman entered with a jangle of gold bracelets, the devilish twinkle in her eyes reflected in the smile on her face.

"Travis!" she gushed, tossing back a sleek fall of mahogany-brown hair. Freckles dusted her nose beneath her tan. Fat loops of gold dangled from her ears. Her dress was a blinding white sheath with a low V neckline and was cinched at the waist with a chamois belt that matched her pumps.

She had an incredibly perfect bosom, Callie noted.

"Janelle." Travis rose. John was a half second behind him. Callie was as frozen as the congressman, glued to her chair in her blue-and-peach plaid shirtwaist and her regular brown leather shoes.

Travis extended his hand, but the brunette was having none of it. She threw herself into his arms.

"Handshakes, la! Is that any way for old friends to reaquaint themselves?" Janelle kissed him on both cheeks, then managed to hold on to him as she shook hands all around during introductions. "Callie, pleased to meet you, I'm sure. John, haven't we met before? At some function or another?"

"Cheyenne Frontier Days, a few years back," John said. "I'm surprised you remember."

"I *never* forget a face or a name." She laughed. "Must come from my political parentage, or is that heritage? What do you think, Father dear?"

Janelle turned to the congressman, who said something Callie didn't quite catch. She couldn't take her eyes off the stunning brunette and the natural way Travis's arm had slipped around her slim waist and stayed there. The sight put a hard lump in her throat.

The meeting, which had already worn itself into a stalemate, ended in a rush of overlapping conversation, with Bob Sealy thanking them all for coming, John pushing hard for another meeting, Travis reextending his invitation for the congressman to visit the CLC, and Janelle inviting herself to dinner. Callie didn't think she could stand it.

Six

"Actually, I just happened to pop by Daddy's office," Janelle explained over glasses of wine at a restaurant known for the size of its steaks, despite its gourmet overtones. "Then when Daddy's aide got nervous, I knew something was up, that he'd been specifically warned against letting me run amok. They always get that same 'bunny in the headlight' look around their eyes, poor boys. So he called Daddy and I sneaked a peak at his desk calendar, and the rest, as they say, is history." She flashed another brilliant smile at Travis. "Goodness knows, once I saw your name, *nothing* was going to keep me cooling my heels in the reception room. Did you know I'm recently divorced?" She lifted both eyebrows in a look of such wide-eyed innocence, Callie choked on her wine. Thankfully, no one noticed.

"No, I didn't know," Travis replied. "I'm sorry."

"Nothing to be sorry about, *cheri*. Arnold was a bore, a rich, safe bore. Daddy felt completely vindicated in his parental duties when he walked me down the aisle. He was sure I'd made the perfect match, and I had, but for him, not me. Of course, you must know it was all on the rebound."

"No, I didn't know," Travis repeated, and tried to change the subject. "Has everyone decided on—"

"But honey!" Janelle interrupted. "You must have noticed the timing. You and I were in Cheyenne together in July, and I was married in October. You remember, the year you won the bareback championship, and Daddy was all over us. Remember? We couldn't shake him? And we were going to elope?"

Travis groaned inwardly and wondered what his chances were of talking Janelle into discussing anything, absolutely anything, other than their very short-lived fling. Not even she could call it a love affair, and he certainly wasn't inclined to embellish the facts.

He'd been a reckless fool those first few years on the circuit, and he'd culminated his foolishness and recklessness in Cheyenne with Janelle Sealy. Elopement, as he recalled, had been decided on after four rounds of dead-dry double martinis—the rage of Washington, D.C., she'd told him, and just the thing to take the starch out of a cowboy's pants, or put it in. He couldn't remember which.

He'd gotten a lot of glory that summer. He was riding so hot, nothing could touch him. The bulls had been rank and furious, the broncs like tornados. He'd ridden them all, and more often than not, landed on his feet and the front page of a newspaper. Fast on the heels of the media blitz had come the Colorado congressman's daughter, looking for a real cowboy and a wild time. She'd found both with Travis.

He glanced at Callie and found her watching him, one brow cocked, both eyes questioning, waiting for whatever answer he came up with to Janelle's claim. He did the best he could.

"I'm starving. Why don't we order dinner?"

Surprisingly, everyone agreed to the new course of action, though only the men actually ate what they ordered. Janelle didn't look the type to take her food too seriously or too often, and Callie was having the same appetite problems she'd been having all spring, thanks to Travis Cayou. The addition of Janelle Sealy hadn't helped matters.

The woman was too much of everything Callie wasn't, like manicured and soft-handed, bejeweled and sheathed in white linen instead of plaid poly-cotton. Callie had hated her on sight purely on principle. Janelle talked a lot, too, and normally that would have driven Callie crazy. But under the circumstances she was grateful someone was carrying the conversation without needing any help from her.

And carry it Janelle did, right into the maw of scandal and back out again with nary a blink. She skirted the shoals of disaster without fear, teasing Travis in ways Callie never would have dreamed up, let alone tried to pull off. She made him blush, and Callie alternated between anger and despair every time he did. The woman was a powerhouse of unleashed female charm—and she only had one hand above the table. Callie didn't even want to think what she might be doing with the other.

"Oh, now Travis honey, don't be shy," Janelle crooned during dessert, giving his thigh a gentle squeeze again. Travis just as gently unpried her fingers again. "You know you were the best. You were *always* the best." She leaned closer, enveloping him within the fragrant cloud of her perfume.

They'd been talking about bareback broncs, but Travis had no doubt that the conversation had taken another one of those embarrassingly intimate turns. He blushed and barely refrained from throttling the lovely Janelle. They'd had some good times, he'd never deny it, but they'd only been good times, nothing more. She'd known the score. As a matter of fact, if he remembered correctly, she'd been the one to explain it to him. If he hadn't been a gentleman, he'd have taken a moment right there at the dinner table to re-explain it to her.

Callie noticed the telltale color rising in his cheeks once more, a faint reddening beneath his sun-browned skin. She bit back another groan and dropped her gaze to her cheesecake. The creamy wedge of dessert was fresh with the taste of tangy lime and floating in a pool of raspberry sauce. Strips of candied lime peel decorated the top, arranged like tiny leaves around a mound of fresh berries. She had never seen anything like it, so perfect, so luscious, and so like lead in her stomach.

The evening was never going to end. She'd figured that out about an hour ago. This was her punishment for unremembered past sins—a never-ending night of continental cuisine and Janelle Sealy. She'd gone past hate and into loathing. Every flash of gold, every tinkle of laughter, every one of his damned blushes wounded her anew.

What a monumental fool she'd become. It was almost too much to bear. Two kisses and she'd lost all reason. She'd known what he was long before she'd met him. How he'd changed her mind about him in less than two months was something she'd rather not dwell on, for she was damn sure it had to do with the sudden searing heat she'd found in his arms.

He'd done his share of work, and more, around the ranch, which was her usual measure of a man. But it was the memory of his kisses keeping her up at night. It was her imagination fooling around with those kisses that made her face turn crimson at the oddest moments. Curran had asked her three times in the last week if she was feeling all right.

She'd lied with a muttered "Yes," but the truth was, Travis's kisses were unforgettable. Being stuck in a restaurant with Janelle Sealy proved the point. The woman hadn't forgotten a thing about him, not one single dang-blasted thing.

"Remember the mechanical bull they had at Laredo's?" she said to Travis. "You won me my very own little bull-riding buckle. It was so cute! I still have it."

Travis was miserable. If Janelle had had a cord on her somewhere, he would have pulled the plug. The woman never stopped talking, especially about him. John didn't seem to mind. On the contrary, the other rancher kept smiling on cue and nodding in all the right places. Callie hadn't smiled or nodded in so long, Travis wondered if she was even listening anymore. He hoped not.

He glanced at her again, his gaze tracing the familiar curves of brow, cheek, and throat, and he felt a tightening in his chest. All he wanted to do was to take her somewhere where he could touch her, where he could caress her soft face with his mouth. It was what he'd planned for the evening from the very beginning. Watching her across the table only made him miss it more.

The candlelight turned her lashes into delicate, shadowy crescents against her cheeks. The color of the flame suffused her skin with a hint of rose gold and put flashes of light into the midnight darkness of her hair. He wanted to kiss her lips and bare her shoulders; he wanted to talk to her all night long while he held her in his arms. And he wanted to hear her voice wash over him with all its husky sweetness.

"I'd never ridden a bull before, of course." Janelle's bell-like tones broke into his moment of reverie, dragging his irritated attention back to her. Her manicured hand rested on the front of her bosom and her eyes were wide. "But I insisted, absolutely insisted. They picked the wildest one and put him in the chute, and I tell you, three men had a hold of me, to get me off really quick, and I sat down there on that *beast* for two seconds! And it was terrifying! I don't know how Travis does it!"

Neither did Callie. Running around with anything in a pair of tight jeans was one thing. Putting an idiot like Janelle Sealy on a bull was another. She'd heard enough. She'd had enough.

"Excuse me," she said, rising from the table with her head bowed, discreetly giving the impression of a woman going to the powder room. That was where she meant to go, but she ended up out in the parking lot, drinking in deep breaths of semifresh city air and wishing she'd never come. Her heart and her pride had taken a beating over dinner. All she wanted was to go home and clear her head of any foolishness she might still harbor about Travis Cayou.

Two minutes later she was headed in the right direction to get her back to the ranch.

Ten minutes after that the guilt started to set in. She really should have said good night, though she doubted if her presence had been missed. It wasn't as if she'd said two words all night. Even John, who had been so glad to see her earlier, had been overwhelmed by a wave of Janelle Sealy charm. Travis had never stood a chance, having once sampled those charms, apparently in abundance.

Lord, that hurt. Her throat tightened and her mouth softened, and Callie knew she was going to cry over him. Nothing out of hand or overly dramatic.

Sad, silent tears would do for a man who'd only kissed her twice.

About half an hour out of town, another feeling crept in on top of the hurt she'd been nursing. It was a niggling thing, like a doubt, but not quite.

She absently brushed a tear off her cheek and concentrated on figuring out what was bothering her—besides not saying good night and being made to feel like a country hick and having her heart broken while nobody noticed. The reason came to her at a spot in the road called Virginia Dale. She'd forgotten something, and that something was Travis.

Stunned, she braked to a slow halt on the side of the highway. Turning off the ignition, she sat in the dark and the quiet, listening to the night sounds coming in through her open window, watching a tractor trailer come over the rise and rumble past in a blur of lights and rolling wheels. Her fingers were clenched and white around the steering wheel, her elbows stiff and straight with strain.

Finally, she looked up through the windshield and out of habit located the Big Dipper and the Little Dipper, as if they could provide a reason for her incomprehensible actions. She couldn't have forgotten him. It was too absurd, too excruciatingly mortifying.

But he wasn't in the truck, and she was halfway home. She took a deep breath and fought back more tears, but the tears came anyway.

With a muffled groan, she dropped her head on the steering wheel and cussed herself up one side and down the other.

John hadn't minded bringing him home, saying Travis certainly would have done the same for him.

John had minded not checking on Callie, but Travis had checked and assured him the truck was in the garage. Actually, it wasn't.

Travis stood outside the back of the barn, looking up the hill at the grove of aspens silhouetted against the full moon. Leaves danced on the wind, filling the night with their rustle and adding a backdrop to the country western song floating down the hillside, coming, undoubtedly, from the radio in the pickup parked under the trees.

It was a good spot to be when a person wanted to be alone with the night sky and the sage. He'd used it himself many times as a teenager, coming home too late, or worse yet, too early. There wasn't anything on the other side of the hill except rolling rangeland and CLC cattle. No lights marred the serenity of the wide, open spaces leading into Wyoming and the mountains.

The passenger door of the truck was open, and he could see the silhouette of her legs stretched up to rest on the open window, one shoe dangling. If he listened real hard, he could hear her voice mixing in with the leaves and Ronnie Milsap.

He dragged his hat off his head and tapped it on his thigh. What was he going to do? he wondered, watching the cream-colored Stetson brush against the dark pants of his suit. With her legs up like that, her skirt had to be down around her lap somewhere, and that didn't do much for his rationality.

Was he going to go up there and talk to her? They had plenty to talk about, like their meeting with the congressman, and their meeting up with the congressman's daughter. Travis had some explaining to do. He was sure of it.

He ought to go up there, if for no other reason than to prove to her he hadn't gone anyplace else. She was probably full of ideas, given to her by Janelle and not very successfully counteracted by himself.

Of course, he didn't have to explain anything to her, but he wanted to explain a lot of things. Like what it had been like that summer in Cheyenne. How great he'd felt. How Janelle hadn't been the only woman dogging his heels, which was probably why she had made such a big deal out of their time together. He wanted to tell Callie what it felt like to be a champion, to have proven something to a whole lot of people, even if most of them did forget your name in a week or two.

He wanted to tell her how winning had eased his homesickness, and how losing had made the loneliness come back hard. He wanted to tell her what coming home meant to him, and what he was beginning to suspect she meant to him.

Was he really going to go up there and talk to her? Just talk to her? He glanced up at the truck and the shapely length of her legs, and he didn't know. But he knew he was going.

Hat in hand, he started up the hill, making enough noise to give her warning without startling her.

Callie heard someone coming, and she knew who it was. Her senses told her. But she lifted up enough to look out the back window anyway, just to be sure. When she saw it was him, she pushed herself upright, facing sideways out the open door with her feet on the jamb and her skirt pulled down tight over her knees, a ladylike pose.

She didn't know how angry he'd be, or even what he was like when he was angry, but she'd prepared herself for the worst. In the process she'd also cleared her head of any fanciful notions of herself and the rodeo cowboy, or the boss of the Cayou Land and Cattle Company, whichever he chose to be.

"Nice night," he said, speaking a few seconds before he reached the truck.

Callie didn't think he sounded very angry. "Nice enough," she carefully agreed.

"Glad you made it home okay."

Well, that was damn generous of him, she thought, watching him come to a stop and lean against the open door. With a single, fluid motion, he tossed his hat onto the roof of the truck, then settled back, the weight off his bad knee, as usual.

"It was an accident," she began, "me leaving you like that. I didn't mean to. I just forgot—" She stopped when he raised his hand.

"No more compliments, please." His smile was wry to match the tone of his voice. "I'm not used to making such an indelible impression on the women I take to dinner."

"You made one on Janelle." The words were out before she thought, but she wouldn't have retrieved them anyway. It was the truth.

Travis bent down and pulled a stalk of meadow grass. He chewed the end for a moment, watching her eyes, what the moonlight did to her skin, the gentle rise and fall of her breasts.

Lord, had he ever seen anything as sweetly erotic as Callie in the moonlight? She'd had the top two buttons of her dress open all day, but now the third button had come undone. He prayed for the fourth to let go, for fate to step in and grant him another little piece of heaven.

"That was a milk cow we had in the chute with Janelle, a Jersey from the petting zoo," he finally said, dropping the grass and scuffing it over with the toe of his boot.

"Oh," she said, her hushed voice noticeably surprised.

"I've done a lot of wild things." He grinned and glanced up at her. "*A lot*. But putting a congressman's daughter, or anybody else looking for a cheap thrill, on a Brahma is way outside my idea of wild. I've been on plenty of bulls, and there's nothing cheap about the thrill of having your arm jerked halfway to Oklahoma, of feeling all that skin you're supposed to be sitting on slipping and sliding over muscles the size of engine blocks. Believe me, if we'd had a bull in the chute, Ms. Sealy would have fainted before she'd gotten a foot on the rail. You've heard them in the chutes, snorting and clanging, and just breathing so loud it's enough to strike terror in the hearts of most people. And I haven't met a bull yet that smelled like French perfume." He laughed and was rewarded with a brief smile. He captured her gaze with his own and his voice softened. "I didn't put her on a bull, Callie, and I didn't ask her to marry me, and four years ago she would have been the one to tell you that the best thing about me was how I scared the hell out of her daddy. Hanging around with a rodeo cowboy was a guaranteed way for a spoiled young lady to get her father's undivided attention."

Callie lowered her lashes and absently pleated the hem of her dress. When she worked up the courage to speak, her voice was a bare whisper. "How did she get your attention?"

"The same way she lost it." She heard him take a step closer, then his fingers caressed the side of her face and his thumb traced a sweeping curve over her cheekbone. "By being everything you aren't."

He tilted her chin up, and his other thumb rubbed across her bottom lip. She felt the deepness of his next breath echo in her breast. Suddenly she was aching for his kiss, to feel his arms come around her.

"Lord, you're beautiful, Callie." His voice was husky, his eyes dark and banked with desire. "The prettiest woman I've ever seen."

His mouth came down on hers, sweet and intoxicating, rough and gentle, unerring. He teased and nipped, then laved her tender skin with his tongue. He easily pulled her to her feet, then just as easily pressed her back against the truck. His body was a hard wall of heat for her to sink into, and sink she did, deeper and deeper under the assault of his mouth on hers, of the thrusting forays of his tongue, of the tension building between them and tightening his body beneath her hands.

She was losing her mind. She was sure of it, but couldn't decide on the path to salvation. Was kissing him guaranteed destruction? Or was it pure sweet ecstasy, the gateway to heaven?

He rubbed against her, with natural ease and perfectly clear intentions. She gasped, and softened, and died a little bit inside.

"Travis," she moaned, dragging her mouth away from his. "Travis, please. I can't . . . I can't do this."

"You don't have to do anything," he assured her, his lips warming the side of her neck while his hand did a slow, skilled slide down the front of her dress, slipping buttons free. "We're just kissing, Callie. Just kissing."

His mouth lifted back to hers to prove his point. She clung to him for a painfully sweet moment, her fingers winding through his silky hair, her lips pliant and yielding under his. He feathered kisses across her face to her temple, the heat of him surrounding her with intangible bonds.

"I don't want to lead you on," she whispered, her tone sincere, her voice breathless. "I don't want to be a tease . . . Please, Travis." His name left her mouth on a sigh as he gnawed a sensually tender path from her jawline to her ear.

He laughed softly against her skin. "It's okay, Callie. You can tease me all you want, any way you want. I'm not going to die from it."

But she might, she thought, especially when he kissed her twice, quick, forcing her head up until her eyes met his. He held her with the heat of his gaze and the promise of his sinful smile, then slipped his hand inside the front of her dress. His eyes slowly darkened and his breath caught before he released it on a muffled groan. "Go ahead, Callie," he whispered. "Tease me."

Run for your life. The warning sounded in her mind, but she was frozen in fear and melting with passion from his touch. Tease him? A thousand images flashed in her imagination, of her mouth tracing a path on him like the one he'd left on her, her tongue dampening his skin, her body growing restless against him in recognition of his overwhelming physicality, her hands trailing down the front of his pants . . . just to tease and feel his response.

She swallowed, and her hand tightened into a fist.

Travis stopped her in mid-motion, his own hand sliding into hers and spreading her fingers. He was losing her.

"Don't, Callie." He held their hands up, tucked between them. "Don't go. Don't worry. Don't run. Everything is okay."

He kissed her brow and watched her lashes lower. He opened her palm against his chest and let her feel the pounding of his heart.

"Everything is okay," he repeated, "except I want to make love to you, and I know you want to make love with me. I can feel it, Callie, in your kiss and the heat of your skin. I can hear it in your breath, and in the soft sounds you make when I touch you. But in one of the wonderfully mysterious ways of a woman, you're saying no."

She started to pull her hand away, but he held her tighter.

"I can accept that, but it's real important to me that we figure out a way for you to say yes. Because when I walk away from here tonight, I'm still going to want to make love to you. And when I wake up tomorrow morning, I'm going to feel the same way. And every time I see you, every time we're alone, in every way I can, I'm going to let you know how much I want you."

She wanted him too. She hurt with wanting him, but if she gave in to the temptation of his loving, she'd be lost.

He released her hand and began buttoning her dress. She tried to stop him and do it herself, but he insisted.

"Let me, please. It may be the last chance I get for a while." There was a hint of laughter in his voice, but it was strained.

When he had her buttoned and hoped she was feeling safer, he kissed her again, sweet and long, letting his mouth savor the taste of her, the feel of her, the softness and the fire. Finally, he pulled away and just held her.

"Lord, Callie, where do you find the strength to say no?" he murmured.

She felt so empty without his kiss filling her. Even in his arms she wanted more. She wanted all of him. "It's not easy," she said, hating the tremor in her voice.

"Then why?"

She thought, trying to put into words the feelings she'd known for so long, the truths she needed to explain. He deserved the truth. What he did to her deep down inside deserved the truth.

"Love is a luxury," she began tentatively, still searching, her head lowered. "Not all love. Some loves are a blessing, like a child, or work that makes you feel glad to be alive. But you, what you do to me, making me want you till I think I might die, that's a luxury." With an effort of pure will and courage, she lifted her chin and met his gaze, knowing only a coward could have done less. "I want you, Travis. I'm probably going to cry all night for not having you. But making love with you would cost me the moon and the stars, and I'm not ready to give them up."

She stepped away from him and started down the hill. He let her get to the end of the truck before he spoke.

"Why, Callie? Why will it cost so much to make love with me?"

She stopped and turned, and he almost went after her. The wind was blowing the skirt of her dress around her knees, and her hair was all tumbled down from their loving.

"Because you don't have honorable intentions," she said, her voice carrying clearly through the night air.

Seven

She was right, of course. He didn't have honorable intentions, or even dishonorable intentions. In truth, he hadn't given his intentions a whole lot of thought, and for some very good reasons. Most notable was, he wasn't sure what intentions she was talking about.

Naturally he had his suspicions, and the strongest of those suspicions didn't bear too much scrutiny. He didn't think she could be talking about marriage. Not that he had anything against marriage. But then neither did he have anything for it.

He hefted the mostly empty spool of barbed wire into the bed of the pickup and signaled to Curran for a break. They'd been mending fences all morning, a job Travis had taken over from Callie as much for her sake as for Curran's. He'd watched the two of them trade off with the post-hole digger one morning till he hadn't been able to stand it any longer. What it took one man a few minutes to accomplish had taken a woman and an old codger about half the day, or at least it had seemed that way. This morning had been much more productive, but even with him providing all of the muscle, Curran was ready for a break and something to eat.

Shoat had gotten creative with the meals lately, and both Travis and Curran opened their lunch boxes with trepidation. It was Callie's fault. She'd been on Shoat's case morning, noon, and night for a change in the menu, complaining she'd be down to nothing if he didn't start jazzing up the meals.

Well, Shoat had sure jazzed them up.

"What have you got there?" Curran asked, doubtfully eyeing the plastic bag Travis had in his hand.

"Stuff," Travis said.

"What kind of stuff?"

"Looks like chocolate chips, and raisins, and peanuts, and pretzel sticks all mixed up together, and some other stuff I'm not sure about."

"We supposed to eat it like that?"

"I think so. It's Shoat's homemade trail mix." He popped a handful in his mouth and gave the older man an encouraging grin. "Good."

Curran rustled around in his pail for a couple of minutes, then asked, "Did you get my sandwich, Travis? I can't find one in here."

Travis looked over the side of the pickup where Curran had spread his lunch out on the tailgate. "It's over there." He pointed. "That round thing. It's called pita, though every time I've had them before, they've been cut across the middle. It's bound to be a little unwieldy in one big circle like that."

Curran muttered something unintelligible, while Travis found his own pita sandwich and used his knife to cut it into a manageable shape. He took a peek inside the pocket of flat bread and another grin broke across his face.

"Damn that old sonuvabitch," Curran yelled, jumping off the tailgate and spluttering bits of sandwich. "What the hell's he trying to do? Kill us all off?" He wiped his sleeve across his mouth. "Don't touch it, Travis. The mayo on that pita sonuvabitch will kill you. It's older than I am. I'm going to shoot the old coot."

Travis took a good bite. "It's not mayo, Curran. It's yogurt-tahini sauce. for the felafel."

"For the what-futel?"

"Felafel. Chickpeas and wheat germ and stuff all mixed together."

His explanation did nothing to take the edge off Curran's upset. The veteran of more roundups than Travis could remember gave him a look of pure disgust. "You mean to tell me I've spent the last twenty years of my life chasing Cayou cattle just so's that old coot can cheat me with chickpeas in my lunch instead of a real beef sandwich?"

"Looks that way." Travis grinned again and took another bite.

"Shoot." Curran swore, then kicked a tire for good measure. He turned on Travis. "You know it's all your fault, dammit."

"Me?" Travis gave him a surprised look, then rallied to his own defense. "It hasn't been me in there complaining about his meals, and I sure as hell wasn't the one who gave him that health food cookbook. I don't even like tofu. Oh no, Curran. If you're looking to lay blame, you're going to have to lay it on Callie's doorstep, not mine."

Curran wasn't buying the innocent plea. "I ain't dumb, Travis. I've seen what's going on, and the only bee in Callie's bonnet is you. She's been strung tight as an I-don't-know-what since the day you got back. I don't know why you don't just take the woman to bed and both let off a little steam. Let things get back to normal around here, especially in the kitchen."

Travis looked at Curran for a long while, chewing thoughtfully. "You know, Curran," he finally said. "I think I'm beginning to understand why you've never been married. You've got women figured all wrong."

"I was figuring out women before you were born, boy, and women ain't changed much. That's the problem with you young bucks. You think you know it all."

Travis laughed. "No, they haven't changed much, not in some ways, I guess, but how many women have you worked for?"

That silenced the old cowboy for a minute. "One," he finally said, then added, "But Callie doesn't act like the boss. She's not one to nag a man to death, or nitpick him till he wished he *was* dead."

"Is she the one you go to when you've got a problem?"

"Well, sure, but that's because James is gone most of the time and even when he's here he doesn't seem to know what's going on anymore."

"And Callie does?"

Curran grinned. "Nothing gets by that girl. Smart as a whip."

"And who signs your paychecks?"

"Callie, when James isn't here. But you're doing it now that you're back."

"Yes," Travis said. "But Callie is still the foreman. Don't fool yourself, Curran. I've been watching her order you around this ranch from one end to the other, you and Shoat both. Why in the hell do you think we're eating felafel? You two just don't know she's ordering you around, because she does it so nice, asking your opinion and taking advice before she gives the orders. But she's giving the orders, don't doubt it. It's her job."

Curran slowly nodded in agreement. "Okay, you're

right on that one, but them's not the ways I was talking about."

Travis knew exactly what he meant. "Yeah, well, ninety-nine percent of all women can't just jump into bed with a man and let off a little steam, and those are the ones you always find yourself wanting. Always," he added for emphasis, then shrugged. "I don't claim to understand it, but it's the God's own truth."

"Hummph," was all he got in reply.

They worked their way through the rest of their lunch in a silence broken only by brief, intensely voiced complaints from Curran that usually took no more than four letters to express. At the end of the meal, when they were loading up to head down to the next strip of broken fence, the older cowboy spoke up once again.

"I could have gotten married. I had my chances, plenty of them."

Travis nodded and tossed a crumpled sandwich bag into his lunch box. "Well, it's a tricky business. Who's to say what's best?" Or what's honorable? he thought. He'd seen some pretty dishonorable intentions crop up in the middle of some marriages. His brother's being a prime example, his own involvement notwithstanding.

Halfway across the greening pasture, Curran asked another culinary question. "What's tofu?"

Travis explained as best he could. "Tonight at supper, when Shoat puts your plate down in front of you? It'll be the white cubes floating in your spaghetti sauce. It's made out of soybeans."

Curran shook his head and cussed for the next fifty yards. "Dammit, Travis. A man doesn't work on a cattle ranch so's he can eat soybeans and chickpeas. You ought to just take the woman to bed."

Travis agreed, but he said nothing. What was between him and Callie was private. Besides, he had too much pride to tell Curran he'd already given it his best shot and all he'd gotten was shot down.

It must have cost a fortune, was all Callie could think as she stared at the huge bouquet of flowers sitting on her doorstep. She pulled her gloves off one finger at a time as she crossed the yard. Why, the delivery charge alone must have been astronomical, more than she'd spent on herself in the last year.

She looked around her as she walked, as if somebody were going to jump out and yell surprise, or remind her it was her birthday, which it wasn't. Baskets of flowers dripping with white daisies and purple irises and pink carnations—and were those yellow roses in there?—did not just show up on Callie Michael's doorstep.

Her strides were cautious as she crossed the dirt road between the ranch house and her private cabin, her boots kicking up feathers of dust. She felt foolish, but her heart was speeding up. Somebody was bound to show up in a minute and tell her it was a mistake. It was ridiculous to let herself get all excited and worked up over a bunch of flowers that somebody had obviously delivered a good twenty or thirty miles in the wrong direction.

The sheer absurdity of her last thought brought her up short. The Cayou Land and Cattle Company was the effective end of the road. There was nothing beyond but a dirt track into the Rawah Mountains that eventually hooked up to a paved road far to the south. No one showed up at the CLC by accident, but she assured herself that stranger things were bound to have happened. The flowers couldn't possibly be for her.

As she got closer, she noticed the tiny white card standing like a flag among the blossoms and petals. Relief and regret hit her at the same time. The card would clear up the mistake—and prove the flowers were a mistake.

The dust settled around her boots as she knelt by the huge moss and wicker basket perched on her small board porch. She wiped her hands with her bandana before reaching for the card. She didn't want to get some other woman's card all dirty. But when she picked up the card and saw the writing on the envelope, it said *Callie Michael.*

Burning with curiosity, she slipped the edge of the envelope between her teeth, picked up the basket with both hands, and hurried inside to wash up. If it was her card—and it seemed it was—she *really* didn't want to get it dirty.

Hands clean, she leaned her hip against the cracked and yellowed counter in her kitchen and slipped the card out of the envelope. *To Callie, with purely honorable intentions. Travis.*

Moving slowly, she turned and sank into one of the chairs flanking her Formica-topped table, her gaze glued to those few words. She read them over half a dozen times, lingering on his name each time. She didn't know what the words meant, or what he meant by using them, or even exactly what she'd meant when she'd said them herself. But they brought an irrepressible smile to her mouth. He'd sent her flowers. And not just any old flowers, but an extravaganza of hothouse beauties.

She laughed and gasped, crushing the card to her chest. Then she buried her face in the blooms, smelling each fresh, exotic scent. He'd sent her flowers.

There was nothing else for it, Travis thought. He was going to have to shoot Curran and Shoat, or hang them up by their heels out in the barn, or get them both married off—which was his least likely prospect, no matter what Curran thought about his eligibility. The two old fools were fawning over Callie as if she were the Queen of England, or rather the Princess of Wales, which might have been bearable if they both hadn't had such appreciative gleams in their rheumy old eyes.

He'd made up his mind. He was going to shoot the next one of them that glanced at her legs, or lingered too long on the neckline of her dress.

He knew the flowers had come. He'd passed the delivery truck on his way back from a run up to Reese Park and Connor's Place. The other two foremen went way back with the CLC, and neither were objecting to Travis picking up the slack while James was away. Jim Kyle had even said he preferred the new order, which had kept a smile on Travis's face all the way home, a smile that had broadened when he'd seen the delivery truck heading back to Laramie.

He'd never sent flowers to a woman before, and given their effect on Callie, he could only wonder how he'd missed their romantic potential. He'd never seen her look the way she did tonight. He'd imagined it quite a few times, but he'd never seen her so aware of her womanliness, almost flaunting her femininity.

Her hair fell in a mass of tumbly waves past her shoulders, loose for a lover's touch. Shorter stray tendrils curled at her brow and temples. He wanted to gather the wild mane in his hands and draw her close.

Her dress was pure seductive innocence, nothing like the practical shirtwaist she'd worn for their visit to the congressman. The material was a navy blue cotton covered in tiny white flowers. The style was old-fashioned, but with modern touches, like the tight bodice with a scalloped edge that skimmed the tops of her breasts, revealing nothing but a promise of what lay beneath. Tiny buttons ran down a lace placket to her knees, a challenge to any man who wanted to free them. Lace edged the capped sleeves and the pockets. She looked delicate and fragile, as if she could melt under his mouth.

"Anybody for more coffee?" she asked. She was standing with her back to them by the kitchen counter, the elegance of her stockinged legs and demure heels mocking her prosaic question.

"Yes," three men answered simultaneously, causing the old fools to chuckle and the young buck to glare at them.

"How about another piece of cake?" Travis insisted more than asked, rising to his feet and picking up the butcher knife lying next to the cake stand.

Let them eat cake, he thought. Lots and lots of cake. Let them spend the rest of the night eating cake.

He began slicing, not waiting for an answer. Double desserts were the norm for Shoat and Curran. Callie never had double desserts, and he was willing to sacrifice a second piece of coconut cake for the chance at an even sweeter confection.

He hadn't had a moment alone with her since he'd gotten home. By the time he'd finished his share of the evening chores, the three of them had been sitting down for supper. She'd looked so pretty, Curran hadn't even complained about the food.

He set the new pieces of cake in front of the two men at the same time Callie set down their refilled coffee cups. Travis wasn't taking any chances. He took her hand the instant she let go of the last cup and led her into the family room, completely ignoring the speculative glances he got from the other two.

"Come on, Callie. I've got something I want to show you." *Something I want to tell you, share with you. Something I need to find out.*

"I don't . . . I mean . . . the dishes. It's my night," she said with obvious hesitation, which he also managed to ignore. He felt as if time were running out, and he didn't want to waste another minute without getting Callie into his life. He didn't give a damn whose foreman she was.

The family room had changed little over the years. The same leather sofas of his childhood were covered with the same Indian blankets he'd always known. The pine paneling had mellowed with age to a welcoming warmth. An old television set with rabbit ears sat in a corner, hardly ever used by boys with hundreds of square miles of ranch to explore. Doily-covered armchairs flanked the largest sofa, situated more to catch the sunsets than the nightly news.

Travis had planned on sitting on the sofa, but when they got to the family room, it didn't seem nearly far enough away from the kitchen.

He continued on to the more formal living room, still holding her hand and pulling her along, but when he got there, he didn't like the looks of it either. He didn't have anything against the chintz sofa, or the little side tables with their delicate lamps, or the shallow bookcase holding his mother's collection of knickknacks and doodads, but he could still hear Curran and Shoat squabbling in the kitchen.

A few more steps took them out the front door to the wide veranda, and there, in the soft, cool darkness of the spring night, he found what he'd been looking for—privacy. Past the old porch swing, down by the southeast corner of the house where the aspen trees crowded close, creating a bower beneath the eaves.

"Thank you for the flowers," she said, barely keeping up with his long strides in her heels.

"You're welcome." He slowed and pulled her up beside him. "I wanted you to have something nice." He slanted her a quick glance as he squeezed her hand.

Callie almost tripped. He never ceased to surprise her. Very few people in her life had ever wanted to make sure she had something nice. Her mother had tried, but out of necessity had concentrated on the basics of food, shelter, and clothing.

There had been special moments, though, special birthdays made so by a mother's love. His words brought back a remnant of the wonder she'd felt on those mornings when she'd awakened to a fancifully wrapped present next to her pillow. As she looked at him, she let herself wonder for the first time if something special was going on between them, something besides her imagination and his kisses.

"They're very nice . . . beautiful." She stammered over the words, trying to tell him how wonderful they were and finding herself woefully inadequate. "Incredible, really. Together they're about the prettiest thing I've ever seen. You must have thought so yourself."

"I haven't seen them," he said. He stopped next to the porch rail and leaned back against one of the posts, still holding her hand. "I called and told them what I wanted, and the lady at the flower shop did the rest."

"Oh." His admission didn't lessen her delight one whit. She just hadn't known how it was done. She'd certainly never ordered flowers from a flower shop.

"I'd like to see them."

"Of course," she said immediately, then hesitated. The request was innocent enough, and she couldn't think of anything she'd like better than for every person she knew to get the urge to visit her while she had a gorgeous bouquet of flowers spilling all over her kitchen table.

Having everybody she knew traipse through her little house was one thing, though. Being there alone, at night, with Travis was another. She wasn't worried about him. It was herself she didn't trust.

The flowers were wonderful, but she knew she'd put on a dress because of his kisses. He made her want to try things she'd always considered dangerous, like needing someone. He made her want to know what it felt like to have somebody special; someone to hold in the night and wake up with in the morning; someone to go out of your way for in the middle of the day, for a kiss or a hug, or just a chat to see how the other was doing. With his dark eyes, hard body, and teasing charm, he made her want a lot.

"Maybe I can stop by tomorrow," Travis said. He'd hoped she'd ask him over tonight, but she'd gone so quiet on him, he hadn't known what else to say.

"Maybe," she agreed softly. Her thumb caressed the back of his hand, gliding over the ridges of his knuckles in a shy gesture. She wanted him and didn't know how to tell him.

The tenderness of her touch wrapped its way

around Travis's heart, making him want to draw her close. He refrained, because it seemed everything she did, every glance, every gesture, made him want to draw her close. He felt like he'd spent half his life since coming home holding her and getting himself all worked up just to have to cool down.

"What did you do before you started working for the CLC?" he asked, hoping idle chatter would keep him sane. He'd read her employment file, the short list of previous jobs and the notes James had taken while checking her references, but he loved listening to her talk, loved letting her voice, so sexy all by itself, wash over him in the darkness. Though it was small compensation for what he really wanted.

"I was a wrangler for a dude ranch up in Jackson," she said. "I worked there for six years, from when I was eighteen, year-round the last couple of years, taking care of the stock in the wintertime when things slowed down."

"Jackson is a fun town," he said absently, returning her caress across his hand with one of his own. "I rodeoed up there a few times. Rode a bronc named Cocklebur into the money one summer. He had a killer trick. He'd buck you out of the chute and then stop dead, like it was all over, and you'd be sitting up there on top of him, seeing your entry fee go down the drain, and cussing and kicking him. Then he'd explode and drop you right into the dirt. Everybody knew about it, but cowboys kept getting nervous during Cocklebur's lull."

"And you didn't?" Callie's voice was breathless, but she couldn't do a thing about it. He hadn't stopped with one caress across her hand. He'd continued on, talking in his easy drawl and turning her hand over to stroke his thumb across her palm and entwine his fingers with hers, intimate and gentle.

"Naw. I whispered a little something in his ear in the chute, got him so riled up he forgot to stop bucking."

"Like what?"

"Nothing I'd tell a lady." He laughed softly and pulled her closer, giving in to temptation and the fascination he saw in her eyes and felt in her racing pulse. His voice grew husky as the inches closed between them and the skirt of her dress pooled against his legs. "You know cowboys, Callie. They'll do things and say things that would make a farm animal blush."

He hadn't planned on kissing her. When he caught her other arm with his hand, though, and she gasped softly and the moonlight shone like silver on her hair, he couldn't remember what he'd planned. Her lips parted and his mouth was on her, that fast, that hot, coaxing and demanding, wanting more than she'd given before. He urged her closer, sliding his leg between hers until she was practically sitting on his thigh, and he felt her shuddering sigh of surrender. He felt the sweet curves of her body soften and mold to his hard edges, and he felt the first stirrings of arousal lick at his loins like wildfire.

"Callie, Callie." He groaned her name as he seared her neck with his kisses. Pulling up one side of her dress, he slipped his hand underneath to cup her bottom. She was wearing a slip, and the silky material bunched and slid under his palm and over the back of his hand, driving him a little bit crazy. The silky things women wore had always driven him a little bit crazy. With Callie the effect was magnified tenfold, with her full breasts pressing against his chest and her hips nudging his without needing his hand to guide her.

She was responding all on her own, turning him on with her soft sighs and the caressing strokes of her hands through his hair. She slowly drew his tongue into her mouth and sucked, once, twice, and he started coming undone.

"Take me home, Callie," he murmured when she stopped the sweet torture, his voice husky with the passion she'd lit like a fuse. He'd understood her silent communication in every fiber of his body. Her invitation had been blatant, provocative—and accepted.

Callie held on to him tight while he stole kisses off her cheek and whispered sweet promises and petitions in her ear. She wanted him so badly, wanted to be held and loved. It was a weakness, she knew, but he made the weakness feel like heaven. She'd spent half the afternoon looking at the flowers he'd sent her, touching each one, inhaling the mingled scents, and falling deeper in love with him with every passing minute. He was a good man, she'd told herself, and she needed a good man.

A loud commotion from the back of the house intruded on their heated interlude like a bucket of cold water. Travis swore and Callie jerked her head around. She'd never heard the sound before, not in two years at the home ranch, but Travis knew what it was. Still swearing, he started running back along the porch. With her instincts as a foreman somehow finding their way through the sensual morass of womanly emotions, Callie followed to find Shoat hanging from the dinner bell, the kitchen door open, and Curran running for the pickup.

"Fire!" the old man yelled, and pointed up the hill toward the calving sheds.

She looked. The rolling hills glowed with an aurora of yellow and orange-gold, mimicking the sunset of an hour before. The grove of aspens was backlit in stark relief against the flaming sky. A shot of pure adrenalin startled Callie into running toward the pickup. Travis was already twenty paces ahead of her.

He swung her up into the bed of the truck when she reached him, yelling to Curran as he did. The old cowboy responded by flooring the gas pedal. He didn't lift his foot once, except to jam the truck into a higher gear.

Eight

They'd moved the herd west a week earlier. Callie thanked the Lord a hundred times for that blessing. The four of them never could have saved the calving sheds if they'd had to wrangle a bunch of fear-crazed cattle. Something would have given way—the fences for sure, more of the calving shed and pens undoubtedly, and probably an extra measure of her nerves.

She'd worked around cattle most of her life. She'd trailed them for more than a few miles, sometimes at a pretty good clip, but she'd never been in the middle of an all-out stampede. Shoat had, and so had Curran, the same one.

"Sixty-eight," Shoat repeated.

"Sixty-seven," Curran said, shaking his head in disgust. "The boys from the Mountain Back Ranch had brought their herd up, and the Mountain Back was busted by sixty-eight."

"Sixty-eight," came the gruff reply.

"Oh, hell, Shoat. I worked for the damned outfit. I ought to know when it went broke."

That the two of them had the energy to argue was

a testament to the toughness of cowboys. She was dead on her feet, covered in soot, parched from the flames they'd fought, and permeated with the smell of smoke, from the scalloped edge of her bodice to the last inch of lace on her hem. She'd changed her heels for a pair of Wellingtons she'd found in the back of the truck, but her feet still hurt.

She leaned over the hood of the pickup, exhausted, listening to the old men and waiting for Travis to finish kicking through the rubble. His succinctly spoken curse stopped the stampede discussion and brought her head up in curiosity.

"Who's drinking McAlister's hooch?" he demanded, holding up a mayonnaise jar half full of liquid. McAlister had never had much success with his cattle, and for years he'd been the local distiller.

The three of them knew Travis didn't think they were drinking the stuff. His question was a request for a current client list of the redoubtable Mr. McAlister. None of them had to think for more than a couple of seconds.

"That sonuvabitch," Curran swore, banging his hand down on the pickup.

"Dammit, Callie," Shoat cussed. "I told you to let James do it. I told you Webster wouldn't take to getting it from a woman."

"James wasn't here," Callie reminded him, her voice firm.

"What the hell are you talking about?" Travis stopped next to the small group.

"Bill Webster, the hand I fired," Callie said. "I let him go the night before you came home. I caught him drinking."

"McAlister's hooch?"

"It was his preferred brand," she said, her tone wry enough to impart her opinion.

Travis looked down at the jar in his hand, not saying anything for a long time. "He could have left the liquor the last night he worked."

Shoat snorted.

Curran wasn't nearly as subtle. "Like he could have left his right arm."

"Is he still around?" was Travis's next question, and an uneasy feeling coursed down Callie's spine. He wouldn't, she thought, knowing damn well he would.

"He was at the Roundup Bar last Saturday night," Shoat said.

Callie could have kicked him. She knew what Travis was thinking. She didn't know how she did, but she did, and it was the exact opposite of what James would have done. James would have called the sheriff.

"Come on, let's get back to the house," she said, rounding the truck to get to the door and verbally heading Travis off at the pass. "I'm going to call the sheriff."

"Don't call anybody. I'll take care of it," he said, reaching around her to open the door for her. "Shoat, you call Reese and Connor's. Tell them what happened and to keep a sharp lookout."

Callie couldn't believe her ears. She wasn't used to having her orders remanded. Not even James did it without first consulting her. Worse yet, what Travis proposed to do ran completely against her management style and beliefs. Even worse, the thought of him tracking down Bill Webster and "taking care of it" made her afraid, afraid for him.

Travis made a move to get in the truck, but she didn't budge an inch. "Go ahead, honey," he said. "Get in the truck."

She froze like a stone pillar, a wave of anger mixing in with her fear.

"Honey?" she repeated, her tone turning the endearment into ice.

Travis always knew when he'd made a mistake, and he knew he'd just made one. But he'd be damned if he knew what it was, and quite frankly, he wasn't in much of a mood to find out. Some bastard had tried to burn down his ranch and in the process had also derailed his night right off the tracks. If he ended up sleeping alone again that night, Bill Webster wouldn't be safe at any distance.

He looked at Callie holding her ground with her chin held high, and he bit off a frustrated oath. An hour ago they had been well on their way to loving each other crazy. After that bit with her mouth all over his, he didn't know how she could take offense at "honey."

"I'm not the *honey* around here," she continued, confirming what he'd just figured out. "I'm the *foreman*, and if I say we're calling the sheriff, then we're calling the sheriff."

Well, he thought, she'd sure cleared up his confusion in a hurry.

"Circumstantial evidence and suspicions are a waste of the sheriff's time," he said reasonably, keeping a leash on his shortened temper. Didn't she see all the implications of the fire, especially if it had been set by someone she'd let go? Even the thought of somebody retaliating against her made him want to break something, preferably that somebody's face.

"I still think we should call him," she insisted through gritted teeth.

"And I think a little talk will probably get my point across quicker and make it stick longer."

"What about *my* point?"

"What *is* your point, Callie?" he asked, his confusion back in full force and acting like a damper on his anger. She mystified him. He honestly didn't know how she could object to him doing any damn thing he wanted. He owned the place, for crying out loud. He reminded her of that, just in case she'd forgotten. "I know you have your responsibilities, but this is Cayou property, on Cayou land, and I don't expect my foreman to stick her neck out to protect it. James had no business leaving you with an unstable drunk for a ranch hand."

Put like that, Callie wasn't quite sure what her point was, either, but she knew he hadn't addressed it. She also knew she couldn't just step aside and let him go. The racing of her pulse wouldn't let her.

"I can't have you undermining my authority with the men. The sheriff—"

"Men?" he interrupted, incredulous. "You mean Shoat and Curran?" He pointed down the hill at the two bandy-legged cowboys, each trying to outdo the other in getting away from what they saw as a purely personal difference of opinion between the two young people.

Callie watched them hobbling along for a minute before returning her attention to Travis. "Yes, I can't have you—"

"Ah, Callie," he interrupted again, a quick grin curving his mouth. "Until I can fill out a pair of jeans the way you do, I don't think you've got a thing to worry about in that department."

Any woman in her right mind would have slugged him for voicing such an unmitigated piece of sexist drivel. Callie was too furious even to think of physical violence.

"How dare you!" she whispered fiercely, her fist

trembling at her side. "I pull my weight around here like any man on the place! I'm up at the crack of dawn, and I don't stop until the last cow is bedded down! Hell! Even if somebody did have a complaint about me, most of the time there's no one here but me to give it to! And you've got the nerve to tell me that the way I sashay my butt around a corral is the only thing keeping Shoat and Curran toeing the line?"

She stopped to inhale before continuing her tirade, but got no further than a quick intake of breath. Travis leaned down and kissed her, hard, pulling her against him.

Despite every ounce of will and common sense and pride she had left, she melted against him. The muscles in his arms flexed around her and his hand slid under her hair, gently gathering the ebony mane into his fist.

The act of capture sparked only a greater need to surrender. She parted her lips on a gasp and felt the sweet invasion of his tongue. His rodeo buckle pressed into her midriff and still she wanted to be closer.

Travis broke the kiss off while he still had a chance, before she made him forget everything except how it felt to have her body soften against him and make him hard, how the scent of her and the feel of her made the world outside their embrace disappear.

"You're right," he whispered roughly in her ear, holding her tight. "I'm the only one who never forgets you're a woman. Never, Callie. Not from the first moment you touched me and called my name."

Lord help her. She'd fallen in love with him. She slid her hands around the back of his neck, holding on to him for dear life.

"Callie," he murmured, brushing his mouth across her temple. "Wait up for me, please."

She stiffened. He was going after Bill Webster. "Don't," she said, hating the pleading quality her emotions lent the word.

"Nothing's going to happen," he assured her. She felt his smile against her cheek as his lips roamed over her face with lazy abandon. "You know I can't just walk away from a man who tried to burn down the ranch buildings. The Cayous haven't held this land for three generations by walking away."

"The sheriff—"

"Can't do anything with a half-empty bottle of hooch, not tonight anyway. We'll have to call him to make the insurance people happy, but we'll do it in the morning, after I've had a chance to set the record straight."

"But—"

"Callie." He shushed her with her softly spoken name. "If it was just you and Shoat and Curran, you all could call the sheriff and be done with it. But I'm here."

She knew what he meant without him saying it. The crime had been against Cayou land, and he was a Cayou. Responsibility and pride were part of his motivation, but there was something more: He cared. He cared about every scorched cinder block and board, and every blackened patch of grass. He had an honor-bound duty to the land and the stock. That's what made him a rancher. She suddenly knew that was what had brought him home, his need for this place, not a couple of wrecks in a rodeo arena.

She also knew James would have called the sheriff. The difference between the two brothers became more glaring with each passing week. James wasn't a bad man, or even a bad rancher, but he was better with the purely business side of the business. He tried to keep his boots clean. Despite his prolonged absences—or maybe because of them—the CLC made a profit every year. But he lacked Travis's tenacity and his passion for the land. James would have seen the burning of the calving sheds as an act of arson, even an act of revenge, but he wouldn't have taken it personally.

She knew Travis took it very personally, like a slap in the face. The danger needed to be neutralized, but the insult also had to be redeemed—personally, not by a man of the law.

"I'll go with you," she said.

"No. If it was Webster, he did it out of anger at you. I can't allow that, and I have to show him he can't get away with it, no emotions involved. Just plain and simple facts. If he lashes out at you or this ranch, I'll break him."

The words, however harsh, were spoken without flair, almost matter-of-factly. They were as he'd said, the plain and simple facts. He'd break any man who hurt her or the CLC.

No, he and James weren't at all alike. And silly girl that she was, she'd gone and fallen in love with Travis, thereby forcing James to fire her from the best job she'd ever had. James wouldn't put up with her, not for a minute, after he found out she was in love with Travis.

"I'll wait up," she promised, and stretched up on tiptoe lifting her mouth to his for another sweet kiss, taking another sure step down the road to ruin.

Bill Webster had not been hard to find. He'd been even easier to intimidate. Travis had done it thoroughly without regrets or second thoughts. The stakes were too high for any half measures.

He hadn't exactly wrung a confession out of the drunk, but he hadn't planned on one. Neither had he extracted any promises, having known enough drunks to realize the futility of such a gesture. But he had put the fear of God and Travis Cayou in the man, and that would be enough, unless Bill Webster found a shred of character in his heart or even half an ounce of courage.

Travis knew good ranch hands had gotten scarcer than cheap money, but James must have been desperate to come up with Bill Webster. He didn't know what James must have been thinking, either, to lighten up even for a second on Bob Sealy. Travis had written the congressman twice and called him three more times since their meeting, and he *had* extracted a promise from Sealy to come and visit the CLC. It hadn't been easy; it had been necessary. The man had forgotten his western heritage and needed to be reminded. James had failed to do that.

He was beginning to think his brother didn't give a damn about the ranch, and he was beginning to wish James would come home, whatever the consequences, just so he could find out. Spring roundup was coming on, and if James didn't make it home in time, he was going to have to go looking for him. He was healed and he was tired of waiting. Some things needed to be settled.

He drove on through the night and the rolling hills, under a sky so full of stars it could make a man's head swim, like one of Callie's kisses. His hand slowly tightened on the steering wheel. Lord, he hoped she'd waited up for him. She'd said she would, hadn't she?

Sure she had, but what if that was all? What if she

just wanted to make sure he got home in one piece? What if he'd read more into her kiss and her words than she'd meant?

She'd said she'd wait up, and he'd heard the buttons on her dress sliding through his fingers. He'd heard the soft crush of her slip gathering in his hand. He'd heard her whisper his name, heard all the sounds of a woman becoming aroused. He'd heard her falling in love and into his bed, and all she'd said was that she'd wait up.

A short expletive hissed between his teeth. He dared not think of her too long, dared not let his imagination conjure her up out of darkness and moonlight to tease him with his fantasies. He'd done it before, a hundred times, and had suffered.

He reached the end of the pavement, and a couple of miles farther he came to the stone arch denoting Cayou land. Off in the distance he saw the light of the yard lamp and the bare flicker of lights in the ranch house. She might have waited for him there, which was fine with him. He didn't have any compunctions about sharing his home or his bed with her. Shoat lived so far in the back of the house, their privacy was secure. As for himself, he couldn't imagine anything sweeter than waking up with her in his bed after loving her all night long, except maybe making love to her again and not bothering to wake up until mid-afternoon.

The pickup rumbled across the bridge spanning the Laramie River, where the road curved back toward the original homestead, and soon he saw the light in a window of her cabin. His pulse suddenly ran deeper and purer in anticipation. His senses heightened, as if a veil of doubt had been lifted.

He couldn't stop his smile. She'd waited up. He parked the truck in front of the main house and walked back across the yard to her cabin. The curtains were closed. When she didn't answer his knock, he tried the door and found it unlocked. He was surprised, and he wasn't. He couldn't remember there ever being a locked door at the CLC, but other than his mom and Beth Ann in the main house, there hadn't been any women either.

Her cabin was like the other two on the ranch. The living room and kitchen were practically the same room, and there was a bathroom and a bedroom. Hers didn't look like the other two, though. Hers was actually decorated, with a color scheme of mostly blue and white, and a style consisting of anything with flowers.

She had wallpaper, blue flowers of a couple of shades on a white background, covering every nook and cranny of wall space in the kitchen area. Unbelievably, the curtains at the two windows, one on the kitchen side and one on the living room side, matched the wallpaper. He hadn't even known a person could do that, but looking at her home, he could see why they might. In a small space, it kept the room from looking all hodgepodge.

A big blue-and-white-striped woven rug covered the brown carpet in the living room, and a small pine-planked bookcase was situated under the window. Her television was on the end of the kitchen counter, facing the couch. And on the couch was a wildly flowered sheet tucked in around all the cushions like a makeshift slipcover—a wildly flowered sheet and Callie, sound asleep on top, curled up in a corner.

Her hair fanned out over her shoulder and the pillow beneath her head, still slightly damp from the shower she must have taken. Deerskin moccasins covered her feet. A blanket was half thrown over her.

She'd changed into a pair of jeans and a white sweatshirt. Not exactly the attire of a seductress, but he couldn't tell it by his reactions, either physical or emotional.

She stirred, and he slowly closed the door behind him, shutting out the night and the rest of the world.

Nine

Travis walked softly across the room, toward the kitchen table and the basket overflowing with flowers. He was impressed. He'd rattled off a vague list of possibilities to the shop lady over the phone, remembering how his mother had liked yellow roses and the irises she'd always cut to bring into the house. The lady had suggested the daisies and carnations, something about simple flowers to soften and integrate the display. He could see now what she'd meant. The basket looked like a well-cultivated yet riotous garden.

He fingered the thornless stem of a half-open rose and bent his head to inhale the scent.

Callie watched him from beneath her lashes, her mind languorous with sleep. Love and longing mingled in her heart as her gaze slid over the purely masculine lines of his body, the long legs, the low-slung jeans riding narrow hips, the dust-encrusted boots of a cowboy working the arid rangeland of northern Colorado. His broad shoulders were outlined against the bright light of her kitchen, adding a rare silhouette to the inside of her cabin and filling her with a sense of security. She stretched slowly and buried her face back into her pillow. Travis was home. She wished he'd hurry up and come to bed. She'd missed him.

Bed? The thought forced her eyes back open. She wasn't in bed. She was on the couch. She stirred again and peeked over at him, trying to organize her thoughts—an impossible feat when he turned and their gazes locked.

Suddenly it all came back to her, his kiss and her promise. He didn't share her bed. That was only in her dreams. She pushed herself up into a sitting position, trying to pull herself together.

"Hi," she mumbled, shoving her hair back off her face and straightening her sweatshirt. She'd been reading a book, hadn't she? Trying to stay awake and wait up for him, because . . . Her thoughts trailed off again and then refocused. Because he'd kissed her senseless once more, on the veranda of the main house and again up by the calving sheds. She squelched a miserable groan and dragged a hand through her hair. She'd left a light on for him to see, so he'd know she'd kept her promise.

"Hi," he answered, his voice soft and deep.

"I made some coffee." She gestured into the kitchen, all the while wondering exactly what she'd promised, or what he might expect from a promise given under the circumstances of her wrapped in his arms under a night sky full of stars. The man wasn't naive, far from it.

"Would you like some?" he asked, taking the short step from the table to the coffeemaker on the counter.

"Sure. Please." She was coming fully awake and starting to feel awkward. They were in her house, but she felt out of place, not knowing whether she should continue sitting on the couch or move to the kitchen table.

He made the decision for her, walking over and setting her cup on the pine bookcase near her end of the couch.

"Thanks for waiting up," he said as he sat down on the other end. "I wish you had come with me. We could have had a couple of dances and a couple of beers. They had a pretty good band at the Roundup."

Her awkwardness disappeared under a wave of irritation, and she pinned him with her narrowing gaze. "Dammit, Travis. I *did* want to come. Remember? You said it wasn't safe."

He shrugged. "Webster was a lot less trouble than I thought he'd be. The man's a weasel."

"I told James that the day he showed up," she said around a yawn with a remaining trace of irritation.

"They why did he hire him?" He glanced at her, his elbows resting on his knees and both hands wrapped around his coffee mug.

"I don't know, I swear," she said, shaking her head. "Sometimes I don't think James cares one way or the other about what goes on here."

The muscles in Travis's arms tensed, tightening his grip on his cup. Her casually spoken opinion unnerved him, coming as it did on the heels of his own similar conclusion.

"I still wish you had been there, even if it was my fault you weren't." He flashed her a teasing grin, ignoring his unease. "You still owe me a date."

"I do?"

"Or maybe I should say I still owe you dinner, since you really didn't eat the last one I bought. Of course, I wasn't exactly up to par that night either, what with all those other people at our table."

"That was also your fault," she pointed out, one silky eyebrow lifting.

He shook his head. "I wasn't the one John had his hands all over."

"He did not!" She was aghast that he had gotten such an impression. "He was only being friendly."

"Too friendly by half," Travis agreed, grinning.

"I've known him a long time," she said, straightening her shoulders and tilting her chin a little higher. "He's always been the perfect gentleman."

"Not like some people you know," he filled in for her, his grin broadening.

She opened her mouth to speak, but no words came. She didn't want to agree with him and bring up a lot of memories of all those kisses; she couldn't play the flirting game and get anywhere except in over her head. But neither could she disagree with him. He wasn't the perfect gentleman, not by a long shot.

He was just perfect, from the sun-bleached streaks in his hair to the darkening warmth in his eyes; from the stubborn set of his chin and the sensual mastery of his kisses, to the way he'd walked into the CLC and proven why his name was the one mortared into the stone arch. She didn't doubt any longer who the ranch belonged to, who the ranch needed more than it needed her—Travis Cayou.

She lowered her lashes, her gaze settling on her rough, work-hardened hands. She'd gotten herself into a stupendous mess by falling in love with him.

Callie inhaled a deep breath and let it out on a long sigh. She knew what she had to do, and the quicker she did it, the quicker it would all be over. She'd kissed him and made a promise she couldn't keep, not now. Making love with the ranch owner was a move too stupid even to contemplate, not the way she'd contemplated making love with a half-wild younger brother, a busted-up rodeo cowboy, somebody who not only searched for thrills but knew how to give them.

Lord, what was going to happen to her? Where was she going to go? She didn't want to go back to just being somebody's ranch hand. She'd gotten used to being the foreman, and she liked the prestige of being the foreman of the home ranch of the Cayou Land and Cattle Company. It was something to show for all her hard work. It proved she wasn't a failure. Falling in love with Travis took all that away from her.

Damn him.

"You've got a lot of nerve," she muttered, pushing herself off the couch. She walked over to the kitchen table and stood with her back to him, one hand on her hip, the other dragging through her long hair.

Pure female, Travis thought, not even bothering to wonder what she was talking about. He was sure she'd let him know when the time was right.

"Some say it's one of my finer points," he replied.

"Men," she huffed, and he couldn't help but notice how the sweatshirt hitched up in the back, accentuating the lush curve of her bottom inside the softly worn denim of her jeans. "You think you can get away with anything."

"Always hoping to," he agreed, letting his gaze roam down the length of her body and back up again.

She whirled around, almost catching him in the act. But he was quick and met her gaze unflinching and unabashed.

"Well, you can't." Her voice was firm in intent and shaky in all the other ways. "You can't show up out of nowhere and start kissing people. My God, Travis.

I *work* for you! You can't ruin my life. I worked hard for this job."

"I thought you worked for James," he said, slowly rising.

"Oh, James!" she exclaimed. "Who gives a damn about James anymore? If you haven't run me off by the time he gets home, he will. I can't win either way."

Travis was starting to get the picture, starting to understand her problem and the way her mind worked. "Run you off, Callie? I've been trying everything I can think of to tie you to me, not run you off."

He didn't understand, she thought, turning back around and laying her hands flat on the table in a gesture of defeat. He couldn't possibly understand, and she couldn't tell him, not about love and commitment, about forever and wedding bands, about having enough guts to stick around for the long haul. A man either knew about those things or he didn't. Men didn't change, no matter how badly a woman wanted him to.

She felt his hands on her hips, sliding up to encircle her waist, and it took everything she had not to lean back into him, into the warmth and solid strength of his embrace. But she didn't have to move. He moved for her, closing the space between them, holding her to him in a highly intimate position that completely undid her.

He buried his face in the curve of her neck, his breath warm and soft on her skin, his body surrounding her from behind. "I see making love with you as a beginning, Callie, not an end. As something we can give each other, not as a taking away."

She turned in his arms, clinging to him and the words she wanted to believe. She'd waited up for him to be held in his arms and seduced by his kisses to the point of no return. No one had ever made her want it more.

Travis gathered her close, lifting her in his arms and heading toward the bedroom. He got no farther than two steps before her soft kisses along the side of his face and neck reminded him of the hasty wash job he'd done before going after Webster. He hadn't taken the time to get the washcloth beyond his collar, and that wasn't right, not when she smelled so sweet in his arms, and not when making love to her wasn't one of those heat-of-the-moment situations he'd found himself in more than once a long time ago, but rather something he'd been dreaming about for weeks.

Without a break in his stride, he turned toward the bathroom. He didn't close the door or turn on the light, and he didn't let her go right at first.

First he kissed her, long and slow, deep and heavy, letting her slide down the front of his body and turn him on with the friction. She hit all his switches with predictable ease.

"I need a shower," he whispered between soft, gnawing bites on her neck as he pulled his shirt out of his pants. "I want you to help me."

Callie tensed, immediately out of her depth. "Travis, I—"

The sound of the snaps on his shirt giving way in quick succession stopped her in mid-retreat.

"It's real easy, Callie," he continued in his persuasive voice. "All we have to do is take our clothes off and turn on the water."

As he explained the seductive simplicity of the matter, she heard his shirt hit the floor and the click of his belt buckle being released. She heard the slide of his zipper and the pounding of her heart.

The dim light easing in from the kitchen filled the

bathroom with a soft glow, shading the curves and planes of his chest and abdomen, showing the hardness of the muscle beneath and the satiny texture of the overlaying skin. He was beautifully sensual, his body crying out for her touch.

"It'll be fun," he promised in a throaty murmur, kissing the corner of her mouth. His hands went to the waistband of her jeans, and her heart went into overdrive.

If he'd hesitated for a second, given her even a moment to consider, she might have stammered her way out of the situation. He did not hesitate. Her button fly slowly but surely opened beneath his fingers, and the longing she'd felt before began building into burning desire.

"Can you help me with my boots?" he whispered, stopping just short of pushing her jeans over her hips. "My knee is still kind of banged up."

"Maybe you're not up to this," she said softly, both concern and disappointment coloring her words.

His short burst of laughter dissuaded her on all counts.

"Believe me, honey. I'm up to it." His arm came around her waist, pulling her close, and his voice grew husky. "I'm up to it all night long with you." His mouth came down on hers in a searingly sweet invasion, his tongue sliding inside to taste and plunder.

Callie could hardly breathe. His skin was so warm beneath her hands, his body a sensual mystery. She wanted to explore all of him, to find the places that made him ache with a need to be touched, the way he made her ache with his thrusting tongue and roaming hands.

He undid the clasp on her bra and cupped her breasts, and she died a little bit from the sheer pleasure of being fondled by him. The pads of his fingers were rough, in contrast to the reverent gentleness of his hands.

"We gotta get these boots off, Callie," he reminded her between kisses. It wasn't absolutely necessary, he knew, and if they didn't get to it pretty quick, doing it with or without his boots on would be a moot point. He broke off kissing completely to pull off the one boot he could, then braced himself in the door frame while she puffed off the other.

Her moccasins took no more than a quick toe-to-heel pressure and a step, and watching her do it gave his confidence a power boost. She wasn't going to run away, a possibility he'd considered and worked to diminish since he'd first carried her into the bathroom.

Which was why he was taken off guard by her hesitation when he removed her sweatshirt. It wasn't much, but enough to make him take his time about it, soothing her with kisses and words, and when the deed was done, with the most sincere appreciation of his mouth and hands.

He'd never seen such beautiful breasts. She was tawny all over, with nipples of a luscious deep brown. He ran his tongue over her, suckling and giving her love bites, and feeling himself consumed by the fire. She moaned and weakened in his arms, leaning into him.

Travis wanted to play with her until the sun rose, wanted to make love with her and learn all of her hidden responses and secret places, but he'd played this first game to its limits. He needed relief. He needed to be inside her, hearing her breath in his ear and his name on her lips, sighing and urging him on. His hands went to her pants, and hers just as quickly covered them.

He didn't mind, truly. He just lost more of his sanity. He took a deep, steadying breath.

"This is going to happen, Callie." The words came out softly harsh, with the barest tremble exposing the depth of his need. "I don't think you can walk away from me, not now, not tonight."

She stood still in his arms, giving him ample time to doubt his conviction and wonder what in the hell he was going to do if she ran off. Then her hands left his, sliding up his wrists and bridging the bare breadth of space between her waist and his. Her fingers wrapped around the waistband of his jeans, and she began to push.

Travis groaned and kissed her lips. "You're safe with me. Nothing bad is going to happen," he assured her in passionate tones. "Nobody wrecks in bed, honey. Making love isn't like bull riding." He paused, slowly lifting his head to meet her gaze, and a purely wicked grin curved his mouth. "Or maybe it is. You'll have to tell me."

She blushed to her eyebrows and beyond. "I'm sure I wouldn't . . . couldn't . . . I've never ridden—"

He laughed and silenced her with a kiss that quickly turned into loving, lingering caresses of his mouth on her body as he removed the rest of her clothes. After he stepped out of his jeans and shook off his last sock, he reached in and turned on the water. He waited while the temperature adjusted, whiling away the time by getting hopelessly lost in the soft fullness of her breasts and the moist promise between her thighs.

When the water was just right and he found himself instinctively pushing against her with every fourth or fifth breath, he led her into the shower.

"Come on, Callie." His voice was husky with emotion and raw with need. "Let me show you how to ride a bull."

The lesson proved sweet almost beyond endurance. Water slickened their skin and ran in sheets down their bodies. His mouth devoured hers with tender carnality, demanding her acquiescence for every instruction.

Callie felt his hands on her body like a brand, searing him into her heart with every caress. He was tough and tender, strong and giving—all the things a cowboy needed to be to win his woman.

When he had her dazed and gasping, aroused to the point of combustion, he slowly entered her. Her head dropped forward into the crook of his neck, nesling there as she let the pleasure of him fill her and take her toward a sensation-drenched oblivion.

Her teeth grazed him as he thrust deep inside. She moaned and opened her mouth again on his skin, tasting the warm man-scent of him, the heat and the clean muskiness. Her left arm slipped around his shoulders to hold him to her, and she felt the muscles in his back bunch and flex with ever increasing tension, the same tension winding through her with dazzling intensity.

Her right hand pursued more practical matters, grasping the top of the shower door for balance and a deliciously rewarding leverage.

"Yes, Callie." The words were torn from him, his face tight with the strain of holding back. His midnight-dark eyes opened and met hers across the steam billowing around them. Holding her gaze, he slowly withdrew and slid back in, then did it again. "God, you're beautiful. Wrap your legs around me . . . yes . . . hold on tight."

His words became murmurings of encouragement and an appreciation she found sorely misplaced.

What he was doing to her with the hard strength of his body and the smoldering heat of his gaze defied description. She'd never felt so alive and so close to death. She wanted the pleasure to last forever, and she wanted desperately for it to end, to end in the place he was taking her.

"Travis." His name slipped from between her lips with soul-wrenched yearning.

He took her then, made her completely his own, covering the peak of her breast with his mouth and urging deep waves of sentient delight over her body, her senses, until she cried out and climaxed around him. The sweet purity of her response pulled at him on levels he hadn't experienced before. The soft pulses of her body plunged him into total, unbounded ecstasy, an absolute release with no direction except deep inside himself. The warm reality of the woman in his arms sent him soaring with emotions more intense than he'd ever felt.

He held her to him for a long time, letting the steam and the water bathe them, letting himself become calm with satiation. He tangled his fingers in her hair and caressed the silky skin of her back as he wondered how long the hot water would hold out. He didn't want to move. He loved the fullness of her breasts pressed against his chest. He loved having her arms and legs wrapped around him and her face resting on his shoulder, her breath heating a small patch of his skin.

Callie was too limp to move. Her muscles were gone, turned to jelly by the man supporting her with unwaning strength. The absolute rightness of their lovemaking had been confirmed by her reaction and by his. She'd picked a fine man to love, more man than she'd ever dreamed of having, and she vowed to tell him so as soon as she found even an ounce of her own strength.

The water turned cool long before she did. Travis carried her into the bedroom, grabbing a couple of towels along the way. They dried each other and collapsed into the bed. Flannel sheets and down comforters cocooned them in luxurious warmth and softness.

His mouth brushed hers with gentle kisses as his fingers stroked damp strands of hair back off her face. He didn't know what to say to her, didn't know how to explain what he felt. He did know he'd found something special in her, with her. He was spending the night, and not because the bed was warm, or because he didn't have anyplace else to go. He wanted to hold her all night long and wake up with her beside him, and he wanted to make love with her again.

His teeth teased the soft fullness of her lower lip, slowly, gently, then just as slowly, just as gently, he began working his way down her body. Before dawn, he would taste her everywhere, feel her every-where, cherish her silky skin with his mouth and sink himself completely into her magic.

Ten

Travis had done a lot of things in women's beds, but he'd never woken up in one and known he was in love. The thought was novel, almost frightening. It was also undeniable. He was in love. He couldn't imagine why it hadn't occurred to him before, except that lust was a much more familiar feeling. He was comfortable with it, knew how to handle it, how to satisfy it or escape, depending on the woman and the circumstances. Love was different.

He raised himself up on one elbow and looked down at the woman lying beside him, so peacefully, beautifully asleep. Her wet hair had dried in a riotous display of curls across the pillows. Her bare shoulder shone with the soft light of dawn filtering through the window.

He wanted to touch her, but he didn't want to wake her, not yet. He wanted to look his fill. He wanted to memorize every line and curve of her face: the feathery lashes sweeping across her cheeks, the pale pinkness of her mouth, the tawny arches of her cheekbones, the dark wings of her brows. She was fiery light and sweet shadows. Her skin glowed. Her hair beckoned for her lover's touch to tame its wildness.

Her lover. Me . . . Travis inhaled deeply as the memories of the night coursed across his mind and down his body.

Love made for great sex. He'd sure learned that in a hurry. He didn't think he'd want it any other way ever again, which brought him to some very interesting considerations, some of which would have had him running out the door with his boots in his hands and his pants barely zipped a month or so ago.

But when he looked at Callie, he didn't want to run. He wanted to stay put, right by her side.

He rolled onto his back and stretched his arms above his head, yawning. He felt great, whole, not tired, not like he'd missed half a night's sleep. Instead, he felt thoroughly rested, as if he'd finally come home. What he'd been missing for so long was a place he'd never known existed, until he'd been in Callie's arms.

The early sunlight of morning edged deeper into the room, reminding him of the one irrevocable fact of ranch life: The cows never slept until noon. His dad had hollered a similar sentiment up the stairs every morning. "The cows are up!" he'd yell, and that meant Travis and James had better get lively.

James. The name lingered in his mind as he brought his arms back down. He didn't know what he was going to do about his brother, but he was getting damn uneasy about what his brother might be doing to him. James had been gone too long not to have something big going on. Bob Sealy was coming at the end of the week, and spring roundup started the next week. He'd give James until after roundup, then he'd get on a plane and go find him.

Until then, though, the cows still needed looking after.

"Callie?" He drew the covers up over her shoulders, tucking them in and gathering her close as she stirred.

She nuzzled her face into the cradle of his arm and shoulder, smiling in contentment.

"I've got to get to work," he said. "I can smell Shoat's coffee from here, and he'll be a bear all day if one of us doesn't show up to drink it."

"I'll go," she murmured halfheartedly and half asleep, cuddling even closer to his warmth.

He chuckled and laid soft kisses along her face. "No, honey. You stay and get some sleep. I'll cover for you."

"Okay," she agreed, whispering the word against his chest.

"Callie?"

"Hmmm?"

"Are you awake?"

"No." She shook her head, tousling her hair into even greater disarray.

"Well, could you wake up for a minute or two?"

Strange man, she thought, strange, fabulous man. He wanted her to get some sleep, and he wanted her to wake up. She sighed and slowly opened her eyes to his smile.

"Hi." He spoke the word like a blessing, the backs of his fingers brushing up her cheek.

"Hi." She smiled in return, so wonderfully pleased with the welcoming warmth she saw lighting his eyes. He had the most beautiful eyes, so richly brown, so gentle and teasing.

"Are you sure you're awake?" he asked, his smile flashing.

"Pretty sure."

"Good. I don't want you waking up later and thinking this part was all a dream, or that I ran out on you in the middle of the night, or that I didn't have enough guts to face you in the morning." His eyes were steady and serious, then a grin twitched the corner of his mouth. "Or that I don't respect you, or that I didn't have a good time, or that I won't be back for more, or anything else you might come up with to worry about. The only reason I'm leaving you is because there's work to be done, and if I stay here as long as I want, nothing is going to get done around here for the rest of the week, because we would both be too damn busy doing all those things we were doing all night long."

It was a lot of words, especially at five o'clock in the morning after a night of very little sleep, but Callie got the gist of it. A small smile deepened the dimple at the corner of her mouth, and a soft blush pinkened her cheeks. They had done a lot of wild things in the night.

"I ought to get to work myself," she said, "or I will think this was all a dream."

"It's no dream, Callie," he assured her in his deep, easy drawl. "I want you to take the morning off. I'll work twice as hard to make up for you not being there. It's a gift, the only one I've got on me this morning, and I want you to take it."

He watched in fascination as her lashes lowered and her blush deepened. Her hand found his thigh and slowly stroked up to his hip with shy but natural ease.

"It's not the only present you've got, Travis," she whispered.

The husky sweetness of her voice washed over him, priming him for love, and her hand did the rest. He never had a chance.

"You're looking a mite peaked this morning, boy," Shoat said as he carried the frying pan to the breakfast table. "Did you have trouble in town last night? Webster give you a working over?"

Travis shook his head and blew on his hands, warming them from the walk across the yard. His shoulders were hunched up around his ears. The toes of his boots were damp with melting frost.

"Wasn't Webster?" Shoat asked.

"No." Travis slid into a chair and tossed his hat on an empty seat.

Shoat stood on the other side of the table, the frying pan in one oven-mittened hand and the spatula in the other, curiosity seeping out of every old pore.

"Must have been Callie, then," he said at last.

Despite himself, Travis grinned.

Shoat chuckled and did a little dance on his bandy legs. "That's my boy. I knew you were a match. Swear to God. I told Curran too." He chuckled again, settling down enough to scoop some eggs onto Travis's plate. "You're probably going to need a tonic. The girl's been alone a long time. I've got just the stuff, a real aphrodeeshiack. Powdered elk antlers. Swear by it myself, and so do the women." He winked and nudged the younger man with his elbow. "We'll get you back in shape in no time, guaranteed."

Travis took the potion in his coffee solely to humor the old man. He didn't need an aphrodisiac. All he had to do was think about Callie and how she'd loved him. He had thought he knew it all, but the range of his experience, he now realized, had more to do with variety than depth.

The tenderness of Callie's touch had done more to arouse him than any amount of practised skill. Her shyness and hesitations had strung him tighter than any deliberate teasing could. She'd whispered words of love, soft murmurings he wasn't sure she'd been aware of, but they'd bound her to him as strongly as he was bound to the land.

He was glad she'd stayed in bed. With any luck, he'd be able to get back there too. Maybe around lunchtime.

He never even made it back to the house for supper. The cows he'd dragged himself out of bed to take care of had conspired against him all day, one of them going so far as to fall off a cliff and break its neck. He and Curran had had to cut down trees to winch it out of the ravine after putting it out of its misery. He was tired and hungry and ached all over, and by the time he got home, there was nothing left in the kitchen but a note from Shoat telling him that his supper was in the oven and his elk antlers were in a cup by the sink.

Travis washed the elk antlers down said sink, letting the water and the garbage disposal run as he stared out the window at Callie's cabin. A light was on in her living room.

He'd seen her twice during the day, once when he and Curran had saddled up their horses, which hadn't given them much privacy for the greeting he'd wanted. He'd settled for hellos and smiles, and a fair dose of frustration. He'd wanted to kiss her so badly. The second time had been when he'd come back for his rifle. Given the state of the cow at the bottom of the ravine, he hadn't dallied long enough for even a taste of her.

Wiping the back of his hand across his mouth, he looked behind him at the empty kitchen, then at Callie's again. He knew where home was.

From inside the steamy confines of the shower, Callie heard him call her name. Her initial rush of excitement and anticipation was quickly doused by disappointment. She'd wanted to look her prettiest when he arrived. She'd already laid out the purple jeans her mother had given her for Christmas, along with the white satin cowboy shirt with pink fringe she'd sent for Valentine's Day. Contrary to what Travis had said, he wasn't the only person in the world who never forgot she was female.

On second thought, she mused, if even half of what he'd told her last night was true, he'd probably like her better just the way she was. She barely had time to blush before he entered the bathroom, barefoot, his pants undone, and already half out of his shirt.

"This could get to be a habit," he said, grinning as he dropped his shirt and shucked out of his jeans.

Faced with his confidence, she couldn't hold on to her embarrassment. He was so sure about the rightness of walking into her life and her shower and making love to her, he was impossible to resist.

Hours later, she admitted resistance had never crossed her mind. She doubted if many women could refuse the pleasure he offered, the sweetness and security, the warmth and strength of him, and she doubted if many had refused him. He was all man, but he had an insight to a woman's needs and desires. He didn't hesitate to use that insight, and when he was unsure, he asked, with teasing whispers and slow caresses until her breath caught in answer.

Before Travis, she'd never known the true lure of passion. Now she didn't know if she could live without it. His body was magic with hers. He was physically addicting and an emotional haven. She loved him—even if he did snore.

The soft rumbling tickled her ear, bringing a tired smile to her face. She'd jiggled him a couple of times for a momentary respite, but anything more woke him, and they both needed their sleep. Despite his proffered gift, she hadn't spent the day in bed. She'd felt too good to stay cooped up. Being outside, working with animals and watching the weather roll in, feeling the sunshine's warmth and the wind ruffling her hair, was what she loved most about her job.

What she loved most about him was everything. She loved where the skin on his arms turned from a coppery brown to pale. She loved the sunstreaks in his hair. She loved what happened to his face when he smiled, how the little boy came out in him when he grinned, and how the man came out in him when he looked at her like a lover.

It was all so new, the thrill of having him close and naked, the warmth of his skin against her, the accessibility of his body, the wonder of waking up in his arms. She knew the thrill couldn't last. She wasn't even sure she wanted it to. How long could she live with such pulse-stopping emotions? She could hardly look at him without wanting to cover his mouth with hers and start pulling his shirt out of his pants. She wanted to back him into corners and tease him until she got what she wanted, and Callie Michael had never fantasized such mischief. Even worse, or even better, he'd made it clear he felt the same way.

They'd gone plumb crazy for each other. She didn't have a doubt about that, but like the thrill, she knew the craziness couldn't last. Something stronger could last, though, something like love, if it was there.

She turned deeper into his sleeping embrace, unwilling to lose a moment of what they had found. He'd taught her how to be a fool for his loving, and she had no regrets. He'd given her the piercing sweetness of his body, and she couldn't walk away. Not from him, not until he turned his back on her, not until he lost the heart for sticking around.

"Stop it, Travis. You can't do that here." She slapped at his hands, then ruined the effect with a giggle.

"It's my barn," he said, reaching for her again. "And my hayloft, and my hay, and I want to play." The last words were spoken in a low growl against the back of her neck.

"Supper's almost ready," she told him, pitching down another forkful of hay.

His answer to that bit of news didn't bear repeating, but it brought a crimson blush to her face.

She tried another tactic, though she wasn't any more inclined to win the argument than he was to lose. "Shoat's expecting us."

"Ah, Callie," he pleaded softly, as if he were truly in danger of being turned down, as if his hands weren't already tugging at her shirt and undoing her belt buckle. "I haven't seen you all day, and it gets lonely out there on the lone prairie."

"You were lonely?" she asked, somewhat incredulous and completely ignoring the fact that he was undressing her.

"Yes," he said emphatically, trying to contain his grin when the snap gave way on her jeans.

"You rode out of here this morning with one congressman, eight staffers, and four other ranchers. How could you possibly have gotten lonely?"

"No women," he said, using a good portion of the sheer nerve she'd accused him of having.

"There was a woman," she reminded him. "The blonde with the congressman. The press release lady or something."

"There was?" He sounded sincerely surprised, and his hands stilled on the fourth button of her shirt. "I don't remember any woman."

"She was wearing jeans, tight jeans, and—"

"Like these?" he asked, rubbing his hands over her bottom and pulling her close.

"Sort of," she admitted, swallowing a sigh. "And she had on a fancy white blouse with a bola, a turquoise bola."

"Oh." His mouth traced a path of heat down her neck as his hand traced a similar path up to her breast. "I didn't notice her. I think you make me lose my mind, Callie."

She was sure of it.

"Besides," he continued, and she felt his grin against her collarbone. "I'm safer here in the hayloft with you than I am in the kitchen. Shoat's trying to poison me with powdered elk antlers."

"Powdered elk antlers?"

"Aphrodisiac."

"Aphrodisiac!" She gasped and pushed away, at least as far away as he allowed her to get, which wasn't far.

"He thinks I need it to keep up with you."

"Travis!" She clutched the open sides of her shirt and pulled them over her breasts. "You told him what we've been doing?"

"I didn't tell him anything. He may be crippled and crotchety, but the man isn't blind, Callie." He pulled her a littler closer. "I've been walking around here for a week all calf-eyed and chomping at the bit. There's only one thing that does that to a man, and that's a woman, and you're the only woman for twenty miles. Honey, anybody could figure out what we've been doing."

"This is terrible. We've got to get down to the house for supper, before he and Curran start thinking . . . thinking . . ." Words failed her. She was mortified.

"Let them think," he said, pushing her hands aside to reveal the lush curves of her breasts. A deep breath swelled his chest. "They could think all night and not come close to knowing what happens to me when I'm inside you."

It was talk like that that melted her senses and kept her in blushes.

"Oh, Travis," she sighed.

"Oh, Callie," he mimicked, flashing a wicked grin.

She lightly cuffed him on the arm. "Don't tease."

"But honey." He dropped back into the hay, pulling her with him. "Teasing you is the only recreation I've had since I came home."

"Recreation?" Her voice rose a degree.

"Sport?"

"Sport?" Her voice and her eyebrows rose a couple more degrees, and she tried again to push away from him. "You should have stopped while you were ahead."

He held on to her upper arms, keeping her close. "Callie, Callie." His voice grew serious and soothing.

"Can I help it if I'm having fun being in love with you?"

"Love?"

He nodded and pulled her nearer, and felt her soften in all the right ways.

"Oh, Travis," she sighed again.

"Oh, Callie," he murmured, still grinning, his eyes alight with promise.

He loved her well and truly in the hayloft, which was a first for Callie. Considering all the actual hay involved, she told him it would also be the last. She was still shaking the stuff out of her braid as they entered the ranch house kitchen. Shoat had left supper in the oven.

"Is it just me, or did the old goat use real hamburger in the meat loaf tonight?" Travis asked, helping himself to another serving.

"It's real," Callie said, and took another heavenly bite. "Mmm, isn't it wonderful?"

"Better than wonderful." He sat down, slanting her a curious glance. "I thought you liked all those new things he's been feeding us."

"The health food stuff?"

He nodded, his mouth full of real beef meat loaf.

"Not really. I bought the book for the vegetable dishes. You know, to get more vegetables into our diet. But Shoat, he's hooked on entrees and starch. So instead of getting eggplant casseroles and zucchini pies, we ended up with chickpea sandwiches and tofu with our pasta and garlic bread. I mean, look at this." She gestured at their plates. "Meat loaf and mashed potatoes. The man hasn't made a salad since I've been here. What happened to broccoli, carrots, cauliflower, green beans?"

"They're all at your house with the lettuce and

tomatoes," he said between mouthfuls. "I found them in your refrigerator."

"You did? When?"

"Last night. I got hungry, so I got up and made a salad."

"You'll eat salad?"

"I love salad." He grinned. "Especially with a baked potato and a thick steak, neither of which was in your refrigerator."

She didn't feel a twinge of guilt. Despite the fare of the last couple of weeks, the man didn't lack for red meat in his diet. She knew he and Curran had barbecued up some beef a few nights ago on a makeshift grill Curran had put together. They'd been out behind the bunkhouse, poking at the coals with sticks, drinking beer, and charring steaks the size of roasts.

"I used to make salads and bring them over for dinner," she said, "but Shoat and Curran never touched them, so I quit."

"Well, we can start again. Or we can just leave the dinner table early every night and tell the old men we're going over to your house to eat salad."

If the size of his grin was any indication, the man thought he was pretty damn clever.

"Oh, that'll fool them for sure," she said, mocking him with a roll of her eyes.

He just laughed and scooped up another spoonful of mashed potatoes.

They ate their cake on the old porch swing, with Callie curled up on one end and Travis doing all the pushing with his long legs. Moonlight filtered through the aspen trees, casting soft shadows across the yard.

"Tell me about Beth Ann," she said, surprising him into a quick stop.

Travis had wondered when she would ask, but that didn't mean he was ready with an answer.

"She was from back East," he said, as if that alone might explain some of Beth Ann's behavior.

"Oh?"

"From what they call a 'good family,'" he added, feeling the pressure to elaborate. "Like some families are better than others, depending on what's in their checking account and where their ancestors came from. Not to say they were rich. They weren't, but I think they thought James was. A couple of hundred thousand acres sounds pretty rich to somebody from back there."

It sounded pretty rich to Callie too. The home ranch was small, but Reese Park went on forever and ran over five thousand head of cattle. Connor's Place was somewhere between the two in size.

"She knew how to ride a horse. I have to give her that," he continued, staring off into the night. He seemed to run out of things to say. Shrugging, he said again, "She was a pretty good rider."

"Was she a pretty good wife?" Callie asked, watching his face.

Silence descended on the porch, but his expression gave nothing away, not regret, or longing, or even memories. After a long moment, he turned and looked at her.

"No, Callie, she wasn't a good wife. And when she was here, I wasn't a good brother. But I doubt if I was as bad as James probably told you."

"Nobody's that bad," she agreed quietly.

"Oh, I don't know about that," he said with a dry laugh, looking away. "If I'd been any younger, or any stupider, I would have been as bad as he thinks, maybe worse. Fortunately, there were a few lines I didn't cross, even if I did trip on them a couple of times. Whatever James says, he has to know I never slept with her."

Callie didn't think James knew any such thing, but she couldn't deny the relief she felt at his self-proclaimed innocence.

"He tried to shoot you. Shoat showed me the hole in the bedroom wall." A damning piece of evidence, and she'd always considered it proof of wrongdoing.

He slanted her a long look. "He was only fifteen feet from me and he missed, Callie. He wasn't trying to shoot me. To tell you the truth, I think he knew more about what was going on than I did. That didn't keep him from *wanting* to kill me. It just kept him from actually doing it."

Callie was silent, partly because she didn't know what to say to that much hate and outrage, and partly because she hoped he'd keep talking, keep explaining. She wanted to know what had happened to tear him away from his home. She wanted to understand, and above all, she wanted to believe.

"You've got to understand how good Beth Ann was," he said, setting his cake aside on the porch rail and clasping his hands between his knees. "It took me months to figure out she was even coming on to me. Everything she did seemed so innocent. I suppose if any other woman had touched me as much as Beth Ann did, I would have gotten the message a lot quicker. But she was James's wife, and I figured it was just her way. Then her clothes started falling off."

Callie stiffened. "Her clothes started falling off?"

He chuckled and slowly lowered his head to his hands, covering his face. "Lord, it was the craziest thing."

She saw his shoulders shake with silent laughter, but she was hard pressed to see the humor herself.

His laughter ended on a deep indrawn breath, and he sat up, resting his arms along the back of the swing. "I've had plenty of time to think it all over"—another round of soft laughter escaped him—"and that's exactly what happened. Her clothes started falling off. Not so much when James was around, but Lord, if it was just the two of us, the woman couldn't keep herself covered. Buttons came undone, shirts fell off shoulders, skirts got hiked up, and jeans got ripped from hip to knee. She should have been a stripper." The laughter faded from his voice. "She was so helpless. She always needed me, and I was dumb enough to like it. Here she was, this sophisticated woman from New York City. She'd done it all, seen it all, and she needed me to get through the day. Pretty heady stuff for a kid who'd spent most of his life looking at the back end of one cow or another.

"One day I ended up in her bedroom, moving furniture or some kind of nonsense. Things got out of hand, James showed up with a rifle, and the old homestead hasn't been the same since."

"You left then?"

He laughed again. "No, I had to stick around long enough to get caught again and get my butt kicked. What James didn't do with the rifle, he almost did with his bare hands. Though the truth was, I was more innocent the second time than the first."

"And she left him anyway."

"She left him anyway. Who knows? If she hadn't had me to work her wiles on and pass the time with, she might have left sooner. She hated the ranch."

"I think James does too," Callie said absently, pushing her cake around with her fork. "Well, maybe not hate exactly, but I think he feels trapped by it. I think that's why he spends so much time away."

"Probably."

"Funny, isn't it?"

"What?"

"You're the one who wants the place, and he ran you off, and he's the one who wants to leave all the time, but he's stuck. He's got to keep coming back."

"Yeah, that's funny," he said slowly, without a trace of humor.

She felt bad for him, the man she loved. He did want the ranch, and they way he worked, she figured he was going to get it. She would stand by him, but there was still James to face, James and a lot of unknowns, some concerning the law and some concerning the heart. She wished it wasn't so.

"Travis?" she said softly, setting her plate down.

"Yeah?" He turned to face her. She was sitting back against the side of the swing, her arms wrapped around her knees. In the pale darkness of the moonlit night, he saw her quick, teasing smile.

"I'm not sure, but I think my shirt is starting to fall off."

He grinned. "Sounds like a job for a cowboy."

"Or a wild bull rider," she whispered, letting her voice go all husky in the way that always set him on the running edge of arousal.

"Come here, woman," he growled. He reached for her hand and pulled her across the swing to straddle his hips.

"Should I run in and get your antler potion?" she teased, settling seductively against him. "Oh, I guess not." Her eyebrows shot upward in innocent surprise.

"I can't get enough of you, Callie." He pulled her mouth down to his, close and touching, but not taking. "The more I have you, the more I want you." His hands tunneled into her hair, working through the dark tresses, loosening her braid, until the waves of ebony silk veiled either side of her face, adding a potent intimacy to the ravishment he plied with the deep strokes of his tongue.

He stole her breath with his kiss, the same way he'd stolen her sense with his body, the same way he'd stolen her heart with the man he'd shown himself to be—not a footloose rodeo cowboy, but a man of duty, stalwart in his claim to the land, a man of integrity, and a man of passion.

He lifted his hips in a slow, sinuous thrust, holding her tight against him, and Callie felt a surge of heat liquefy in her veins. He groaned deep in his throat.

Passion . . . The thought trailed across her mind as the sensation itself suffused her body with heated need. *Definitely, undeniably, a man of passion.*

Eleven

Callie crossed the yard from the barn, mildly curious at the sight of a sleek gray Cadillac parked in front of the ranch house. It wasn't the congressman's. His fancy car had been blue.

She pulled her leather work gloves off and slapped the dirt off her thighs, in case the Cadillac's owner was someone she needed to talk with.

That was unlikely, she realized when she saw Travis ride up at a ground-eating gait. He halted at the back porch and swung out of the saddle, letting the reins trail to the hard-packed earth, ground-tying the horse. In four long strides he disappeared inside the kitchen door, slamming it hard enough for the noise to carry across the yard. Something was up, and she'd bet anything it had to do with the gray Cadillac.

Travis was the boss. She'd conceded the honor and the responsibility to him without question. But she was still the foreman, and there were some things he didn't know about, like the arrangement she had with the veterinarian, and the credit she had coming from the farrier.

Of course, neither Doc Morrow, the vet, nor Judd Thomas, the farrier, drove a Cadillac, but there were other situations that might need her input and expertise. She'd better go inside.

The house was quiet when she entered, surprising her. With all the noise Travis had made getting in, she'd expected an uproar of some kind or another.

She got it before she was halfway across the kitchen.

"No!" a man shouted, the voice coming from the front of the house. "Not this time, *damn you*. Not this time. She doesn't want to see you."

She heard Travis's voice, but she couldn't make out what he was saying. Concerned, she strode into the family room, then under the arch that led to the more formal living room and the ranch office.

"He's yours," she heard the other man say. "I checked it a dozen ways to Sunday, and the facts add up. *What in the hell were you thinking?*" He stopped speaking and cussed a blue streak, punctuating his tirade with what sounded like his palm landing on the desk. "You *weren't* thinking. You never thought. That was always the problem. I'm so *damn* tired of taking on your responsibilities."

Something in the man's inflection stopped Callie cold in her tracks. She knew that voice. James was home.

A rush of adrenaline poured through her system, feeling very much like fear and lasting all of a moment before she conquered the unreasonable reaction. James had hired her; he didn't own her.

But he did own a new Cadillac, she thought with teeth-gritting irritation. His sense of priorities had always galled her, especially when it shorted the ranch.

Travis spoke again, his words intensely quiet and

damnably unintelligible to Callie where she was standing by the chintz sofa. She had no such problem with James's next outburst.

"Damn you, *you lying son of a bitch.* I should have shot you when I had the chance." Violence seethed beneath each syllable, compelling Callie into action. The gun case was in the office. She had to stop whatever was going to happen before one or both of them remembered that.

She made her steps loud and firm across the oak floor, her boot heels echoing in sharp but unhurried cadence. "Travis," she called.

The only answer she received was his dark, piercing glare when she entered the office. She tore her gaze away to face the other man.

"James." She nodded slightly and took another step inside the room, halting next to one of the leather armchairs fronting the desk.

"You should have told me he was back, Callie." James's tone was accusing and red-hot with anger. Sweat had beaded on his brow and dampened the graying darkness of his hair. He stood behind the desk, his eyes cold, his fist wrapped around a half-empty bottle of expensive Scotch. A small paunch hung over the cowboy buckle holding up his charcoal-colored slacks.

"He owns half this ranch. I couldn't have kept him off," she said coolly, trying to force him to reason and hoping he hadn't really drunk half the bottle.

"Couldn't . . . or wouldn't?" James demanded, holding her steady gaze with his own. Then he turned away with a snort of disgust and a bluntly spoken curse. "He's had every woman from Santa Fe to Cheyenne. He's had my wife, and now he's had my foreman. I never took you for a cheap piece, Callie. Get your gear and get out."

"You bastard." Travis stepped forward even before the full impact of James's words had sunk into Callie's mind.

"Bastard?" James whirled to face the younger man, his face livid. "The only bastard in the family is the one you got on my wife!"

Shock rocked Callie back on her heels. She clutched at the chair, her fingers digging into soft leather, her gaze riveted to Travis.

He glanced at her, then looked back at his brother. "Get out of here, Callie. This is going to get a whole lot worse before it gets any better."

Unlike James, Travis seemed in perfect control, deadly, calculated control. She didn't want to leave them to their mayhem, but neither could she stop it. She needed Shoat. He would know what to do.

Releasing the chair, she took two steps backward, then turned and ran, the word "bastard" ringing in her ears.

She checked the garage and half the outbuildings before she spotted Shoat repairing a gate latch on the far side of one of the corrals.

"Shoat!" she hollered, skidding to a halt in the middle of the dusty road. "Get to the house! James is back, and they're at each other's throats!"

She didn't have to say it twice for him to get the full picture. Arthritis aside, he hobbled toward the ranch house with Callie half lifting him off the ground with the strength of her grip around his arm. She shoved him through the kitchen door the same way a lion tamer might toss a piece of meat to his cats. He was her peace offering.

"You stay put, gal," he commanded, knowing as well as she that her presence would be more hindrance than help. She was fresh fuel on an old smoking and acrid fire just looking for an excuse to blaze out of control.

She backed away from the door, wringing her hands together until she realized what she was doing and dropped them to her sides. There hadn't been a shot. She would have heard a shot. In between the confusing repetition of "bastard" and other remembered snatches of the conversation, she'd kept her senses honed for the sound of a shot.

She paced the back porch, forcing herself to wait, her ears straining for sound from the front of the house. The minutes passed and nothing happened, and slowly the confusion of her thoughts started settling down, sifting out, organizing into neat compartments. Thoughts like *"He's yours"* and *"the bastard you got on my wife."*

Travis had a son, an illegitimate son, seven or eight years old. At least James thought he did. James had checked out the facts, and checking facts was James's specialty.

But Travis hadn't slept with Beth Ann. He'd slept with every woman from Santa Fe to Cheyenne. He'd slept with the foreman. But he hadn't slept with the woman who'd had him so tied in knots that even being shot at in her bedroom hadn't scared him off.

Of course he hadn't. He'd said he hadn't. He had no reason to lie . . . unless he had a son he didn't want to claim.

Callie kicked at the mud-scuffed porch, angry with her doubts and even angrier at herself for thinking them. She hadn't asked him for particulars; he'd had no reason to lie to her.

But she'd been called a bastard herself. Long before she'd known what it meant, she'd heard the word thrown in her direction and not liked the sound of it.

What in the hell was going on in there? She turned back to the kitchen door and peeked through the window. She couldn't see a thing.

The sound of another door slamming jerked her attention away from the kitchen. She hesitated for only a second before running to the side of the porch to see her worst fears realized. Travis was leaving. He opened the hood of the Cadillac first and pulled something out. Then he jumped in the ranch pickup and tore off in a cloud of dust.

A thousand emotions collided in her chest, disbelief and a sense of betrayal, and the fear that James had been telling the truth. Why else would Travis have run?

She squeezed her eyes shut so tight, she saw lights dancing. Damn him. Damn him.

Get your gear and get out . . . I never took you for a cheap piece . . .

As quickly as that, she didn't belong. As quickly as that, she was homeless and unemployed. Suddenly she was trespassing on the porch she'd painted last summer. Suddenly the horses in her string weren't her horses. They were Cayou horses, and she was standing on a Cayou porch, and the only damn thing that could have saved her was the damned Cayou driving hell-for-leather in the opposite direction.

Get your gear and get out . . . He couldn't have said it any plainer, and she at least had enough pride to take him at his word. James had never given her any reason not to take him at his word, drunk or not.

Another terrible thought struck her. When he saw the payroll and her increased salary, he might think she'd tried to steal from him.

Her hand tightened into a fist, and she barely refrained from slamming it against the porch rail.

For all his faults, James had been right. Travis was nothing but trouble.

Nothing but trouble and the man she loved.

She'd tried packing slow and she'd tried not packing at all. Neither had made her feel any better, so she'd gone ahead and packed everything real fast. She hadn't left, though, if only because the only way she could get from the ranch to the bus station in Laramie was in the pickup truck, and Travis hadn't come back with it.

She knew she was pushing her luck hanging around so long, praying Travis would come back and save her. Being fired off the CLC wasn't a drawn-out affair, and James had shown up on her doorstep once already, yelling for her to get out and calling her names no decent woman should have to hear. She'd done her evening chores anyhow, then she'd cooked her own supper, avoiding the ranch house kitchen. Soon after, Shoat had arrived with half a chocolate cake, no word of Travis, damn little advice, and Curran with a deck of cards.

"Gin." She spread her cards out on the table and left Curran to count points and mutter. With James on the rampage and the coil wires ripped out of his new car, they were all hiding out at her cabin, waiting for Travis. She was hoping that when he came back, he'd miraculously settle everything, prove he wasn't the father of Beth Ann's son, and convince James not to fire her. If that failed, then she'd ask someone to give her a ride to Laramie, where she could catch the bus to Cheyenne and her mother. But as she waited she was dying inside.

In truth, dying was putting it lightly. Her whole life was crumbling down around her ears. It was all she could do to keep from wearing a hole in the carpet, pacing up and down and back and forth, going rigid with anger and swearing.

Forcing herself once more to a show of relaxation, she leaned her chair back on two legs and watched Curran count under his breath. She even took a sip of coffee without her hand trembling. She had no idea how she was keeping the tears back. That was a miracle.

She brought the chair back down on four legs and glanced over at Shoat while she gathered up the cards. He'd kept himself posted by the window most of the evening, and for a talkative old coot he'd been unnaturally quiet. The deck riffled through her fingers in a smooth shuffle, bringing her attention back to the game.

"Sure you don't want to play, Shoat?" she asked, arranging the cards in her hand.

"Nope."

"Well, don't wear out the glass in the window." She brought her gaze back to her cards, thinking she should have been an actress.

In the next minute the sound of an approaching vehicle blew her nonchalance all to hell. She was out of her chair and at the window before Shoat had a chance to draw the curtain back. She ripped it aside and instantly recognized the ranch pickup.

"I get first shot at him," she muttered, whirling to leave, her emotions jumbling together in relief and anger.

A hand on her arm held her firmly. "Better not, Callie," Shoat said, his voice gentler than his grip. "Let me go and get everybody settled."

"Everybody?" She narrowed her gaze and pinned him with it. He'd been holding out on her all night.

She'd known it from the start. "You know where he's been, don't you?"

"I'll send him over," Shoat said.

"Don't bother," she snapped, turning back to the window. "He knows where I—" She stopped abruptly, her breath caught in her throat, her anger frozen by a stab of quick, icy pain.

Travis had gotten out of the truck with a woman and a boy.

"I didn't know for sure, Callie," Shoat said softly behind her. "I didn't know for sure that he'd find them, or that James was telling the truth 'bout them being in Laramie. Lord, she hated it so much eight years ago, I never figured her for coming back, especially with such a cockamamie story as the one James has been spouting all night."

Callie ignored him. "The card game is over, Curran," she said, her voice tight and strained.

Curran grabbed at the chance to escape what he feared was coming, namely tears. He'd never been any good with a woman's sniffling, and he doubted if getting on in years had improved him much in that area.

"'Night, Callie, Shoat." He left the cards, but picked up his cake plate and squeezed between the two of them to get out the door.

The worst day of her life, Callie thought. This was going to go down as the worst day in her life. Him running off was one thing. Seeing him with that woman was another.

She quickly took in the incredibly sophisticated and oh-so-casual flow of Beth Ann's richly colored watered-silk slacks, the discreet outline of shoulder pads under the matching blouse, and the bluish-bronze sheen of her high-heeled pumps. But mostly her gaze stuck at where Travis's hand met Beth Ann's elbow.

She didn't even know Shoat had left until his silhouette blocked the other two adults from view for a few seconds as he crossed the yard. She shifted her position to keep them in sight, watching the small crowd mount the steps to the broad front porch. The yard lamp lit the area with a golden glow against the black velvet night.

Within that circle of light, one head shone with a short crop of silvery blond hair. The boy. Callie felt her heart tighten as he turned for a moment, his face illuminated, along with a myriad of emotions. She didn't recognize any of Travis in the young face, but she did recognize the uncertainty and the fear drawing his features tight. For all of her love, her mother hadn't been any good at providing security either. She had done her best, and Callie faulted her for nothing. But the scars were there, and the emotions she saw on the young boy's face rubbed against them.

She jerked the curtain closed and pressed her fist against her mouth. She was a grown woman. She was in control of her life. James could fire her, but he couldn't break her. Only Travis could do that, and she wasn't ready to face that right now.

Dropping her hand to her side, she strode across the kitchen and into the bedroom. She didn't allow even a twinge of regret or doubt to cross her mind. If he wanted her, he could come find her, but she wouldn't stay to be a bone for two brothers to fight over. Let Beth Ann have that honor.

She hauled her suitcase off the bed. It held all of her clothes and a couple of pictures she'd had hanging on the walls. The large box with her personal items was already in the living room. All told, it didn't look like much for two years' worth of living in a place, but she'd spent most of her time outdoors or up at the main house, and the cabin had come fully furnished.

Ten minutes after Travis had driven up, she had her stuff loaded in the back of the truck and was knocking on Curran's door. It only took one sad and lonely tear coursing down her cheek and half a sniffle to convince him to drive her into Laramie. She had a lot more trouble stopping crying than she'd had starting, and by the time they hit the highway, she knew Curran wished he'd been stronger back at the ranch.

"There, there." His voice was gruff as opposed to the ineffectual pats he was giving her shoulder. He reached into his back pocket and handed over his handkerchief.

She wiped her eyes and blew her nose, and sobbed a few more times until she was able to get herself under control. After a moment of silence another sob broke through, then another, and she was at it again.

"There, there." He reached down into his boot and drew out a small flask. "Have a shot, boss. Buck up."

She accepted the flask and unscrewed the top. Her first sip laid a hot trail down the back of her throat, and the second reached all the way to the pit of her stomach. She gasped and tightened her grip on the flask, pressing herself deeper into the bench seat. But she didn't cry.

Curran figured he was on a roll and pulled a tin of tobacco out of his other back pocket. "Chew?" he asked.

She shook her head. Curran helped himself to a pinch and they rode in blessed silence for the next half hour, with Callie nursing the flask and Curran spitting at the mile markers.

"Damn fool," Curran said as a car streaked by, taillights blinking and horn honking.

The car pulled up in front of them and immediately began slowing down, holding them to the road.

"Sonuvabee," Curran whispered, using a politer version of one of his favorite words for Callie's sake. "We're being hazed by a Cadillac."

Travis was so furious, it was all he could do not to slam on the brakes and take his chances with getting rear-ended by the pickup. He'd had a hell of a night, a regular hell of a night. James had a string of pin-striped investors lined up from Boston to New York to Washington, D.C., all of them hot and heavy to turn the CLC into a damn Disneyland of condos, resorts, retreats, and dude ranches. The only thing standing in their way was Travis, and the only thing on his side was that James hadn't expected to find him standing quite so close.

James had thought a little long-distance black-mail in the shape and size of a seven-year-old boy wrapped up in a paternity suit would be enough to scare him off. Or maybe Beth Ann had come up with the idea. Travis didn't know and he didn't care. The two of them were in cahoots, but that was their problem. There was no way on God's green earth they could prove the boy was his, because the boy wasn't.

From the looks of him, he wasn't James's either, which meant Beth Ann must have been a whole lot busier than either one of them had guessed. They'd had a wrangler on the CLC back then with white-blond hair and baby-blue eyes. He'd been a good hand, but without two nickels to rub together he couldn't have held Beth Ann's attention very long.

All of this had steamrolled over him in the last five hours, and then Callie had run off on him.

He could hardly believe it, but one look inside her cabin had confirmed the worst of his fears when he'd seen the pickup gone. She'd taken James's word over his. She'd taken James's command over his love.

He was furious.

He stopped the Cadillac with the pickup nosing close behind, and car doors were shoved open in quick succession.

"Howdy, Travis," Curran said.

"Curran." Travis's voice was curt. He strode by the ranch hand without a glance.

"If you can teach that thing how to cut like Babe, you might really have something there," the old man called after him, chuckling.

Travis came face to face with Callie by the tailgate.

"Where do you think you're going?" he asked, louder than he'd meant and with his arms flying high in the sky as if he'd just finished tying a calf.

"To my mother's," she said distinctly, giving the impression of thinking each word out.

"Your mother's? In Cheyenne? For a visit?"

"Yes . . . yes . . . and no." She took her time formulating the answers to his questions, then she stumbled, without moving an inch.

Travis caught her, holding her up by both arms. "You're drunk," he said between his teeth.

"No."

"You're coming home with me, right now."

"No."

"Why not?"

"I won't be your handy whore."

Travis stared at her, dumbfounded. Then, very

slowly, he leaned her up against the tailgate to keep from trying to shake some sense into her.

He clenched his fists and tilted his head back at the sky, inhaling a long, deep breath. He was getting a headache, a killer, and it was her fault. He squeezed his eyes shut. *Handy whore.* Where in the hell had she come up with a term like that?

She stumbled again. Without looking, he caught her with one hand on her shoulder and held her steady while he thought. He didn't know what to do.

"Callie," he began, opening his eyes and drawing on his last ounce of patience. "It's been a bad day. Come home."

"Damn right it's been a bad day. I've been fired, cowboy." She leaned against his steadying hand and drawled the last word in his face, as if it were an insult.

He was angry enough to take offense at the truth. "Cowboy, is it? Cowboy?"

"Yeah." She leaned farther into him.

"Great. Fine. Cowboy." He released her and started to back away, but the instant he moved, she slipped. He caught her on the downfall and jerked her up close. "So help me, Callie. If you think being fired is the worst thing that happened today, you don't know the half of it."

"I saw the half of it, both halves, the one in silk and the other scared outa his mind." She held her shaky ground with her chin in the air, refusing to be intimidated.

"Beth Ann? This is about Beth Ann?" He didn't believe what she was telling him. She couldn't possibly be jealous. It didn't make sense. After all they'd shared, how could she possibly think he would run off after another woman?

But her chin jutted out more. "I saw you holding

on to her, helping her up the porch like she couldn't get to the damn front door on her own. I saw you." She hiccuped. "You never hold on to me to make sure I get up the damn steps."

Travis swore and tightened his grip. "The day Kathleen Ann Michael needs my help to get anywhere, I'll be there, holding on for dear life. With Beth Ann it was either hold on to her arm or wrap my fingers around her throat. And considering all the other problems I've had dumped on me today, strangling my brother's ex-wife didn't seem like a good idea."

"She's pretty." Her voice took on a sad tone, and Travis knew he was losing her.

"You're beautiful." He gave her a little shake to keep her from passing out. "Come on, Callie. Let's go home."

"No, no, no. I can't go back. James said he won't have any handy whores on the place."

Furious, Travis realized, was a relative term. He'd been upset with Callie, and a shade angry with Beth Ann for her latest tricks and lies, but he was furious with his brother. Mind-jarringly furious. James would be eating the words "handy whore" on his knees in the dirt before Travis was through with him, and it would be Travis's dirt. He'd sworn himself to that.

"Curran. Get over here." He gathered Callie in his arms, relieved she didn't have enough spunk left to argue. If James wanted to fight down and dirty with him, he'd take him on with no holds barred. Callie was a different matter. He wanted her out of it.

"Yes, boss?" Curran asked, rounding the truck.

Travis held her with one arm and pulled a wrinkled up wad of bills out of his jeans pocket. "Take her to Laramie. Get her a hotel room, someplace nice. Nothing cheap. Does her mother know she's coming?"

"They've been on the phone real regular tonight," Curran said, accepting the money Travis shoved in his hand.

"Good." He turned his attention back to the woman in his arms. "Callie?"

"Hmm?" She snuggled closer.

"Go on to your mom's like you planned. All I ask is that you stay put where I can find you. Okay?"

"Okay." She didn't sound nearly sure enough to suit him.

"And don't worry about getting fired off the ranch. If James has his way, in a couple of months there won't be anything left of the CLC except a fat bank account with his name on it. In order to stop him, I've got to stay on the homestead, right in the house, stake my claim and prove to him and his investors that I'm more trouble than they can handle and still be profitable. It's the damn holy grail to their kind—profit."

Slumped against him in cozy comfort, she nodded her head, making him wonder if she was hearing or understanding anything he was saying.

He slipped his arm between them and grasped her chin, tilting her head up. "Stay put at your mother's, Callie," he ordered, wishing her eyes were open so he could get a reading on her. "When I come for you, I don't want to have to track you all over Colorado and Wyoming."

Another slight nod and a little humming noise were all he got in answer.

He thought about kissing her, then he thought about where kissing her usually led him, and finally, reluctantly, he decided against any such rash action. Making love on the side of the highway didn't seem appropriate behavior with the woman he'd decided was going to be his wife—if he didn't come out of this fight flat broke, busted, and looking for a home. He wouldn't ask any woman to share that kind of life.

So instead of kissing her, he hugged her hard and felt all the frustrations of the nights to come. Then he helped her back into the cab of the pickup and waited at her window until Curran was behind the steering wheel.

"I want you to stay with her until she's on the bus," he said.

"Yes, boss."

"And then I want you back at the home ranch, reporting to me, no one else."

"Yes, boss."

"And Curran?"

"Yeah?"

"Don't give her any more liquor."

Curran chuckled and started the truck. "Yes, boss."

Twelve

Two weeks. A lifetime. Callie dragged the brush through her hair for the last time and tossed it next to the bathroom sink. It was Saturday night, and she was going out. Her mother had insisted. She and her accountant fiancé had tickets to the local dinner theater, and she didn't want Callie home alone all night. Three of Callie's friends from high school had insisted. They'd been calling her all day to make sure she wasn't going to back out. Finally her broken heart had insisted. She couldn't coddle herself forever. Travis was gone out of her life. He'd paid Curran to put her on a bus, and she hadn't seen or heard from him since.

Still, it had taken two weeks for her heart to break. She remembered, or thought she remembered, what he'd said to her that night on the highway, about staying put where he could find her, and about James trying to sell out the CLC, and it was roundup. She knew he had his hands full.

Of course he has his hands full. Beth Ann is at the ranch. A mocking voice inside her head wouldn't leave that particular fact alone. She glared at her reflection and picked up the brush again to give her hair a couple more swipes.

He hated Beth Ann, she told herself. The woman was a snake. She was trying to make herself rich by destroying the one thing Travis wanted more than anything on earth—the Cayou Land and Cattle Company.

Of course he wants the ranch. It's irreplaceable, unique, not at all like a foreman, or a lover. She forced herself to hold her own gaze and not let her mouth tremble. She hated herself when she was like this. Sarcasm didn't make losing him hurt any less.

She'd tried calling him, waiting a few days between each attempt. But that woman kept answering the phone, and once even James had answered. She hadn't said a peep to him, but she'd steeled her pride and left messages three or four times with Beth Ann.

And of course Beth Ann drops everything and runs right out to tell him. Probably not, she admitted, but she wouldn't have thought he'd need reminding to call her.

She dropped the brush again and straightened the collar on her white satin cowboy shirt with the pink fringe. Her mother had loaned her a pair of silver concho earrings. The bright buttons of metal glittered against her dark hair. Her purple jeans were snug fitting and flattering, cinched at the waist with a hand-tooled leather belt. She looked good, good enough to go out and kick up her heels on a Cheyenne Saturday night.

Dammit, she didn't want to go out. She wanted to stay home curled up on her mom's sofa, watching old movies and wallowing in her misery a while longer. She wasn't ready to start over.

A sigh lodged in her throat. She blinked a few

times to keep from giving in to tears. She'd known better. She'd known better from the start, but she'd still gone ahead and fallen in love with him. Now she had to pay the price she'd always known was there.

Heartache was to be expected when a woman took up with the likes of Travis Cayou.

Callie's mood didn't change in the next few hours, but the number of people witnessing it had multiplied exponentially as she and her friends had traveled from her bar to bar, saving the loudest and busiest for last.

"Callie!" Julie, a perky, petite blonde, yelled close to her ear, trying to be heard over the rocking and rolling country-western band and the din of a few hundred people carousing. "That cowboy is coming over again. This time you have to say yes, or he won't ask you to dance anymore."

Callie took a quick look over her shoulder, confirming what her friend had just said. A tall dark-haired man was weaving his way from the bar to their table, a big smile on his face, his expensive hat at a jaunty angle.

"He's no cowboy," she said, turning back to her beer. She'd noticed his hands the first time he'd asked her to dance. They looked like they'd never held much more than a cordless phone and a mechanical pencil, and the angle on his hat was scandalous, if not outright silly. She hoped he understood her turning away. She didn't want to have to tell him no again.

"Well, hell." Julie sighed and rolled her eyes. "If you're going to wait for a *real* cowboy to ask you to dance, we might as well give up now and call it quits."

Callie brightened for the first time all night and started to agree, but Julie cut her off.

"Oh no you don't. Melinda and Joan are having a great time, and I'm not leaving until I'm having a great time too."

Actually, Julie had turned down at least as many offers to dance as Callie had, and so had her other two friends, whenever either one was the only one left at the table with her. Callie thought it was sweet, but unnecessary. They didn't need to babysit her. She was old enough to take care of herself in a bar, even a wild one like the Pioneer Club and Saloon.

For all the people present, the music and noise provided its own brand of isolation. Julie only spoke when she noticed something exciting or interesting, and Callie hardly spoke at all, letting her attention drift over the crowd of two-stepping bodies and the sea of hats.

She needed to start looking for a job. She should have started two weeks ago, when she'd first arrived in Cheyenne. She was sure the big ranches had already hired for roundup, and she didn't fancy working for a two-bit cow-and-calf outfit. She'd been spoiled by her work on the CLC.

She could always go back to dude ranch work, and maybe that was her best bet. Her credentials as a wrangler were impeccable, whereas she didn't even have a letter of recommendation from James for her three years working on the CLC.

Julie's hand wrapping around her upper arm and jerking her close startled her out of her reverie.

"You wanted a cowboy, girl?" Her friend's voice was bubbly with excitement. "I'll bet a dollar to every dime you've got in your pocket that the real thing just walked in the door."

Callie didn't doubt it, not considering the western

crowd already filling the bar, but the appreciative, flirtatious expression on Julie's face prompted her to go ahead and look over her shoulder. Julie was a woman whose head wasn't easily turned.

But then, the man standing in the one clear space at the far end of the bar had been known to turn quite a few heads, from congressmen's daughters, to cheating wives from New York City, to cowgirls working the range. There had to be a few barrel racers and break-away ropers among the ranks too. The women on the rodeo circuit couldn't have been immune to Travis's sweet charm and teasingly potent sexuality. Callie certainly wasn't.

Her heart pounded painfully in her chest. He looked exhausted, ragged, and worn-out. Dust clung to his denim shirt and his jeans, a pale veil over work-softened indigo and the darker places where hard dirt had been ground in, and noticeably non-existent where he'd been protected by his chaps. Sweat stained the band of his hat. Weariness and the broadness of the western sky had feathered lines at the corners of his eyes.

He was all cowboy, from the unmentionable dirt on his boots to the beat-up Stetson pulled straight and low across his brow. She stared unblinking at him for heartbeat after heartbeat while he stood at the end of the bar, visually searching the room for someone.

He hadn't seen her yet, and she was tempted to make a run for it. She wasn't sure her nerves or her knees could hold up to a meeting with him after two weeks of silence, especially in a public place. But the cowardly thought no sooner crossed her mind than his eyes met hers, cutting across the haze of smoke and the tumult of people. The dark intensity of his gaze held her as he crossed the bar with long,

purposeful strides, his easy grace belying the tired
ness etched into his face.

He was coming for her, and she could do nothing
but hold her ground and wait.

With all the noise in the bar, he didn't even
attempt to speak until he had her pulled out of her
chair and held tight against his chest. Callie caught
just a glimpse of the shock on Julie's face before
Travis claimed her undivided attention.

"I miss you," he said, tangling his hand in her hair
and holding his mouth close to her ear. His other hand
stroked the length of her back and circled her waist,
his words and actions giving her all the reassurance
she needed, but not nearly as much as she wanted.
She was in love, and he'd left her for two weeks. He had
a lot of making up to do, a lot of hurts to soothe.

She nodded in reply, holding on to him, letting him
know she missed him too. Oh, how she'd missed
him. Her whole being soaked up the flood of security
she felt with his strong arms around her.

"I can't stay long. I've got to be back at Reese cow
camp by roll-out." His voice was rough with longing,
smoothing to a whisper as the band took a break.

She nodded again, still not trusting herself to
speak. She'd held on to memories and fragments of
love, afraid she would never have anything else,
afraid that James had been right and she'd been
convenient. She couldn't have borne that kind of
shame.

But he'd come for her, if only for a short while. She
hated his news, but welcomed the sentiment behind
it, knowing he must have ridden hard and driven
even harder to get to her tonight.

Then something strange tugged at the part of her
still very much a foreman, the part of her waiting for
something to be wrong, the one part of her not

all-woman, melting in his arms and hoping he'd stay long enough for them to make love and for her to tell him she didn't think she could stand it if she couldn't be with him.

"Reese?" she asked. "What about the home ranch? Who's bossing my roundup?" She angled her head back, confusion knitting her brows. If Travis was at Reese, then the home ranch was not only shorthanded, but virtually without a leader. Shoat couldn't sit a horse all day, and Curran, though more than qualified, had never shown any interest whatsoever in taking charge of anything.

"The home ranch is gone, Callie. I'm sorry." His hands tightened around her waist. "James had it sold before he ever came home. They brought some-body down from Montana to liquidate the herd. He's probably running the roundup and getting all the calves branded, but I don't know what brand they're putting on them."

"James sold the homestead?" Her voice was soft with disbelief. "He sold the house your granddaddy built?"

"It's the prettiest place of the three. The man who bought it wants to make it into a dude ranch. He's going to keep a few cows for authenticity, but the rest of it's gone."

"He can't do that, Travis," she insisted, her voice shaking now with realization of just how much was wrong, despite his coming for her. "Your name is on the title; it has to be. He can't sell it without you." She was angry and hurting for him, and for herself. She'd loved the home ranch like her own.

"You're right, he couldn't do it without me. I let it go." A certain harshness edged his words; a certain grief flared in his eyes.

"No." She jerked out of his arms.

He grabbed her right back, holding her tight. "I fought for Reese, Callie. For something we could make a living on, and without Bob Sealy backing me up, I doubt if I could have gotten away with as much as I did. James had it all figured out, the payoff, the lawyers, and the loopholes. He'd written me off and convinced a lot of other people to write me off too. It was a done deal by the time he came home, Callie. The home ranch was gone, and I didn't think it was worth losing Reese Park to get it back."

Hard reasoning, but Callie knew he spoke the truth. There wasn't room for sentiment when a man was fighting for his life. But she felt as if someone had stolen something precious from her.

"Connor's Place?" she asked.

"Gone. To a group of those pin-striped investors."

"What about Jim Kyle and Everett Shaw? What are they going to do?"

"Shaw is going with the new buyers, at least until they figure out what to do with the cattle he's running. Considering there isn't a one of them who's ever seen a steer on the hoof, that might take quite a while. They wanted the land for an investment. Kyle will stay at Reese for as long as I can keep him."

"And Shoat? And Curran?" The two old cowboys didn't have anything without the home ranch. They'd both thrown their lots in with the Cayou Land and Cattle Company a long, long time ago.

"They'll come with us, Callie, to Reese."

"Us?" she whispered.

His hand slid down to the base of her spine and pressed her close while a fiery darkness lit his eyes. "I miss you," he growled under his breath.

She blushed crimson at the way his body moved suggestively against hers.

He chuckled, his eyes still gleaming. "I know this

may be hard to believe right now, but it's more than sex."

"Oh, sure," she teased, still not knowing what to make of what he was saying.

"I signed the papers on Reese last night." His tone grew serious, to match the sudden intensity of his gaze. "I want you to come home with me, to my home. I want you to be my wife."

There was pride in his voice and possession in his words. Callie caught at her lower lip with her teeth to keep from crying, but it didn't work. She buried her head against his chest, wetting his denim shirt with her tears. He'd lost the home ranch, but he'd won, too. He'd won a future for them to share.

The year she'd spent at Reese had been good. There'd been something special about riding across so much land, knowing it all belonged together, something she'd missed at the home ranch. The barns and outbuildings at Reese were an oasis in the middle of an endless expanse of prairie, all of them anchored by the two-story ranch house. When riding the range, she could see the house from miles away. Old and weathered and solid, the house had withstood winter storms and summer heat for fifty years. It would stand for another lifetime of love for her and Travis.

"Callie honey." He wrapped his arms around her and rocked her. "You've got the rest of your life to cry over marrying a broken-down rodeo cowboy."

"That's—that's not why I'm crying," she managed to choke out between sniffles and sobs. She didn't know what was wrong with her. She'd never been the crying type. She'd always been sensible, low-key, as steady as the day was long—until she'd met him, and he'd turned her into more woman than cowpuncher. With Travis as her man, she lauded the change. "I love you, Travis Cayou."

"I know. I could tell that first day in Laramie, in the bus station. You couldn't keep your eyes off me."

"I didn't love you then," she said, looking up at him and wiping away a fresh tear.

"Maybe not," he conceded with a grin. "But you wanted me."

"I didn't even know you," she insisted, her eyes widening and her blush returning.

His grin broadened. "This sounds like an argument I'd like to have in bed somewhere, anywhere, with you, tonight, before I have to be up at the crack of dawn to rawhide cattle all day. We've got just enough time to get home, make love, and grab an hour's worth of sleep. Or maybe we could forget making love and grab a couple of hours of sleep."

"No," she said, her blush deepening but her voice holding firm. "I don't think we should skip that part."

"I think you're right." He cupped her face in his large, weather-roughened hands, strong hands to hold a bull or a bronc with hard-won skill, or the woman he loved with tenderness. "What you give to me, I need, Callie, all of it, from making love to making our life. We've got a ranch to build, a legacy to care for and pass on. I want my children with you. I'll take good care of you." He slid his arm around her waist, holding her tight, and a slow, easy grin curved his mouth. "And all I ask is that you have enough guts to stick around."

"I do," she promised, knowing he was making his promise to her.

"And that you'll respect me in the morning," he added, his grin growing wicked.

"I will," she assured him with appropriate solemnity.

"And that you won't take off with the next good-looking, wild rodeo rider to come down the pike."

"Never."

His grin slowly faded. "Then I'm taking you home, Kathleen Ann Michael. To have and to hold." His mouth came down on hers, with sweetness and tenderness, and with passion, sealing his vow with a kiss.

THE EDITOR'S CORNER

There's a kind of hero we all love, the kind who usually wears irresistible tight jeans and holds a less-than-glamorous job. The world doesn't always sing his praises, but the world couldn't do without him—and next month LOVESWEPT salutes him with MEN AT WORK. In six fabulous new romances that feature only these men on the covers, you'll meet six heroes who are unique in many ways, yet are all hardworking, hard-driving, and oh, so easy to love!

First, let Billie Green sweep you away to Ireland, where you'll meet a hunk of a sheep farmer, Keith Donegal. He's the **MAN FROM THE MIST,** LOVESWEPT #564, and Jenna Howard wonders if his irresistible heat is just a spell woven by the land of leprechauns. But with dazzling kisses and thrilling caresses, Keith sets out to prove that the fire between them is the real thing. The magic of Billie's writing shines through in this enchanting tale of love and desire.

In **BUILT TO LAST** by Lori Copeland, LOVESWEPT #565, the hero, Bear Malone, is exactly what you would expect from his name—big, eye-catching, completely fascinating, and with a heart to match his size. A carpenter, he renovates houses for poor families, and he admires the feisty beauty Christine Brighton for volunteering for the job. Now, if he can only convince her that they should make a home and a family of their own . . . Lori makes a delightful and sensual adventure out of building a house.

You'll get plenty of **MISCHIEF AND MAGIC** in Patt Bucheister's new LOVESWEPT, #566. Construction worker Phoenix Sierra knows all about mischief from his friends' practical jokes, and when he lands in an emergency room because of one, he finds magic in Deborah Justin. The copper-haired doctor is enticing, but before she will love Phoenix, he must reveal the vulnerable man hiding behind his playboy facade. You'll keep turning the pages as Patt skillfully weaves this tale of humor and passion.

Kimberli Wagner returns to LOVESWEPT with **A COWBOY'S TOUCH,** LOVESWEPT #567, and as before, she is sure to enchant you with her provocative writing and ability to create sizzling tension. In this story, Jackie Stone ends up working as the cook on her ex-husband's ranch because she desperately needs the money. But Gray Burton has learned from his mistakes, and he'll use a cowboy's touch to persuade Jackie to return to his loving arms. Welcome back, Kim!

There can't be a more perfect—or sexy—title for a book in which the hero is an electric lineman than **DANGEROUS IN THE DARK** by Terry Lawrence, LOVESWEPT #568. Zach Young is a lineman for the county, the one to call when the lights go out. When he gets caught in an electric storm, he finds shelter in Candy Wharton's isolated farmhouse. He makes Candy feel safe in the dark; the danger is in allowing him into her heart. All the stirring emotions that you've come to expect from Terry are in this fabulous story.

Olivia Rupprecht gives us a memorable gift of love with **SAINTS AND SINNERS,** LOVESWEPT #569. Matthew

Peters might be a minister, but he's no saint—and he's determined to get to know gorgeous Delilah Sampson, who's just moved in across the street from his Iowa church. He's as mortal as the next man, and he can't ignore a woman who's obviously in trouble . . . or deny himself a taste of fierce passion. Once again, Olivia delivers an enthralling, powerful romance.

On sale this month from FANFARE are four breathtaking novels. **A WHOLE NEW LIGHT** proves why Sandra Brown is a *New York Times* bestselling author. In this story, widow Cyn McCall wants to shake up her humdrum life, but when Worth Lansing asks her to spend a weekend with him in Acapulco, she's more than a little surprised—and tempted. Worth had always been her friend, her late husband's business partner. What will happen when she sees him in a whole new light?

Award-winning author Rosanne Bittner sets **THUNDER ON THE PLAINS** in one of America's greatest eras—the joining of the East and West by the first transcontinental railroad. Sunny Landers is the privileged daughter of a powerful railroad magnate. Colt Travis is the half-Indian scout who opens her eyes to the beauty and danger of the West . . . and opens her heart to love.

INTIMATE STRANGERS is a gripping and romantic time-travel novel by Alexandra Thorne. On vacation in Santa Fe, novelist Jane Howard slips into a flame-colored dress and finds herself transported to 1929, in another woman's life, in her home . . . and with her husband.

Critically acclaimed author Patricia Potter creates a thrilling historical romance with **LIGHTNING**. During the Civil War, nobody was a better blockade runner for the South than Englishman Adrian Cabot, but Lauren Bradly swore to stop him. Together they would be swept into passion's treacherous sea, tasting deeply of ecstasy and the danger of war.

Also on sale this month, in the hardcover edition from Doubleday, is **SINFUL** by Susan Johnson. Sweeping from the majestic manors of England to the forbidden salons of a Tunisian harem, this is a tale of desperate deception and sensual pleasures between a daring woman and a passionate nobleman.

Happy reading!

With best wishes,

Nita Taublib
Associate Publisher
LOVESWEPT and FANFARE

Don't miss these fabulous Bantam Fanfare titles
on sale in JULY.

A WHOLE NEW LIGHT
by Sandra Brown

THUNDER ON THE PLAINS
by Rosanne Bittner

INTIMATE STRANGERS
by Alexandra Thorne

LIGHTNING
by Patricia Potter

And in hardcover from Doubleday,
SINFUL
by Susan Johnson

A WHOLE NEW LIGHT
by
New York Times bestselling author
Sandra Brown

Cyn McCall knew she could always count on her late husband's friend and business partner, Worth Lansing. He could always make her laugh and forget her problems—she could tease him about his many romantic entanglements. The last thing Cyn expected was to lose herself in longing for a man who could never settle down.

When Worth invited his best friend Cyn to a getaway weekend in Acapulco he never suspected that he'd respond to her the way he did to any beautiful woman. While he thought it was time she stopped mourning and moved forward with her life, he couldn't escape the feeling he was betraying Tim's memory. But guilt couldn't stop the rising tide of desire threatening to overwhelm him.

Cyn wanted to believe that their night of abandon was sparked by the exotic locale and intoxicating scent of hibiscus. Worth knew they shared something deeper, a passion that would outlast the Mexican sunglow . . . if only Cyn would open her heart to new possibilities and the promise of love.

THUNDER ON THE PLAINS

by
Rosanne Bittner
bestselling author of
IN THE SHADOW OF THE MOUNTAINS

It was a time of enormous turmoil and far-reaching expansion for America. The Civil War and the assassination of a President had torn the nation apart, but one man's great vision—of building a transcontinental railroad that would join the East and West could reunite it. Bo Landers's lifelong wish became his daughter's destiny.

Sunny Landers was utterly devoted to her father's dream . . . until she met Colt Travis. And she knew, with the searing shock of a lightning bolt, that he was the only man she could ever love, though their worlds might separate them.

Half Cherokee, but raised by whites, Colt Travis was like the vast, rugged land of his birth: handsome to gaze upon, yet wild, imposing, and dangerous. When he first laid eyes on the spirited, passionate daughter of Bo Landers, the man who'd hired him to scout into the Western territories, he knew she was everything he'd ever want in a woman . . . but believed he could never have.

"It's getting almost too hot," Colt told Sunny. "You sure you don't want to go back?"

"No. Not yet."

"Just be careful you don't let the sun burn that pretty face."

She laughed lightly, lifting the canteen and drinking some more water. She offered it to him, and Colt met her eyes. He swore if he didn't know her better, she was giving him a look of invitation, but he was not about to take that road. It could lead to nowhere but disaster for both of them. What in God's name was this all about?

The woman was to be married soon! What the hell was he doing out here in no-man's land, riding with the richest woman in the country, a woman who dined with presidents and owned half of Chicago and dished out millions like pennies, a woman who was part owner of the very company for which he worked? This was the most absurd situation he had ever encountered! He took a swallow of water and handed back the canteen, then reached behind him to get out tobacco and a cigarette paper.

"That's the scar from when you were wounded by the Pawnee, isn't it?" she asked, her eyes resting at his right side.

Colt rolled himself a cigarette. "It is. I've finally managed to put all that behind me."

She began undoing her braid. "Where do you go from here, Colt?"

He lit his cigarette and took a deep drag. "I don't know. I guess I'll wait and see where life leads me. I've pretty much always done it that way." He removed his hat and hung it, too, around the saddle horn by its string. He ran a hand through his long dark hair, then turned to tie his shirt into his gear, the cigarette still in his mouth. "How about you? Why are you doing this, Sunny? You should be back in Chicago, making plans for a grand wedding, not out here riding like a wild woman who's scared to death of her future."

Sunny looked away, wondering if he knew what seeing him bare-chested did to her—his dark skin glistening in the sun, that cigarette between those full lips, those gentle hazel eyes. He was raw power, so sure, so handsome, so forbidden. "Who said I was scared?"

"Nobody. It's just written all over your face, that's all. Does it have something to do with marrying Blaine? You think you're going to find some kind of answer out here?"

She shook out her own hair, enjoying the feel of letting the long blond tresses fall free. "I don't know. I've never been sure about Blaine, and yet I should be." She sighed deeply. "I should be the happiest woman in the world right now. I have everything . . . everything." Her voice trailed off.

"That depends on what *everything* means. Look at what you have compared to me, and I pretty much feel *I* have everything, yet you could buy and sell me a million times over."

She stared off at the higher bluffs on the horizon. "No, Colt. No one buys and sells someone like you. You're your own man. You aren't impressed by money, and you don't judge people by it. That's why I feel so good when I'm with you, in spite of how hard it is for us to be just friends. With you I don't have to put on any airs, pretend I'm something I'm not."

"Do you pretend around Blaine?"

"Sometimes." She met his eyes. "I'm sorry. I know this is hard for you, and that I promised to let you go on with your life and me with mine. I know it's best we have absolutely nothing to do with each other, but when I think of never seeing you again, or even being able to write you, or—" She looked at him pleadingly, her eyes tearing. "Once I marry Blaine, it really will have to end. That's why I had to come out here, Colt. It isn't fair to you, and it makes no sense at all; but I felt almost led out here against my better judgment." She reached back and took a deep breath. "Now I don't regret it at all. This has been the most wonderful day I can remember since when Father and I came out here and he let me ride with you. It's strange, isn't it, how people move in and out of each other's lives—how some things change so much but other things stay the same, like the land. When I come out here it's as though the last ten years never happened. "

Colt smoked quietly for a moment. "But they *did* happen, Sunny. I lost my best friend, a wife, and a son; you lost your pa and became one of the most powerful women in this country. I've been through a war and a hell worse than death in that prison camp while you became part owner of a transcontinental railroad and built another grand home and offices in Omaha—became engaged to a man whose wealth probably matches or tops your own. My life has been one of tragedy and pain and dirt and sort of going on from one pointless thing to another. Yours is filled with balls and boardrooms and diamonds and soon a wedding that will make the papers in other countries. Things *do* change, people grow apart, especially those who have no business being involved in each other's lives."

She fought the tears, realizing what he was telling her. He could not be a part of her life. It was like that night at Fort Laramie, a gentle good-bye, a painful lesson in what was right and wrong. But she also remembered Vi's words about following her heart, about how love could conquer great obstacles. Did Colt believe that? She sniffed and wiped her tears, refusing to look at him.

"Dammit, Sunny, don't cry. I told you that ten years ago." He took another long drag on the cigarette, suddenly feeling awkward. He had spoiled her happy day. *Damn her!* he thought. How many times had he said that to himself? God, he loved her, and that was the hell of it. Should he tell her? How could it possibly help anything? It would only make everything worse.

She straightened in her saddle, retying her canteen. "I'll always treasure our friendship, Colt. One thing no one can take from me is my memories, or my dreams." She held her chin higher and faced him. "I'll race you," she told him.

"What?"

She gave him a daring look, a new boldness in her eyes. "I said I'll race you. If you catch me and manage to pull me off my horse, you've won!" She charged away, and Colt sat there a minute, wondering what she was up to. What was this sudden change in conversation? She was like a crazy women today, and she had turned his feelings a thousand different ways.

He watched her, the way her bottom fit her saddle, the way her hair blew in the wind. Her daring look stirred his pride, and the race was on. He kicked Dancer into a hard run, manly desires stirring in him at the challenge of catching her. He held the reins with one hand and smashed out his cigarette against his saddle horn with the other, tossing the stub aside, and leaning into the ride. "Get up there, Dancer," he shouted to the horse.

Dancer's mane flew up into Colt's face as he galloped up and down more sandhills. He noticed Sunny veer to the west rather than north, and he turned Dancer, taking a cut between two more sandhills and emerging near Sunny as she came around the end of one hill. She screamed and laughed when she saw him, and now he knew he could catch her.

He came closer, the determination to reach her now a burning need. It went against all reason, was totally foreign to all sense of maturity. They were like children for the moment, and yet not children at all. The emotions it stirred in him to think of catching her were dangerous, yet he could not stop himself. He came ever closer, and now he was on her!

Sunny screamed when she felt his strong arm come around her. Suddenly, she was free of her horse and sitting sideways on Dancer, a powerful arm holding her. She covered her face and laughed as Colt slowed his horse. "Now you are my captive," he teased.

She threw her head back and faced him, and both of them

sobered. For a moment they sat there breathing heavily from the ride, watching each other.

"We had better go catch your horse," he finally told her.

"We'll find it later," she answered. She moved her hands to touch his powerful arms, ran her fingers over his bare shoulders. "Tell me, Colt. What does an Indian do with his captive?"

For a moment everything went silent for him. Nothing existed but the utterly beautiful woman in his arms, her tempting mouth, her open blouse, her blue eyes, her golden hair. He moved a hand to rest against the flat of her belly. "He takes her to his tipi and makes her his slave," he answered, his voice gruff with passion.

She touched his face. "That's what I want you to do with me, Colt. Make me your slave—today, tonight, tomorrow."

He shook his head. "Sunny—"

She touched his lips. "Don't say it, Colt." Her eyes glistened with tears. "I don't know what's right and wrong anymore, and today I don't care. I just want you. I've always wanted you." A tear slipped down her cheek. "It can't be anybody else, Colt, not the first time. I—"

His kiss cut off her words, a deep, hot kiss that removed any remaining inhibitions. She could barely get her breath for the thrill of it, the ecstasy of his hand moving to her breast, the ache of womanly desires that surged in her when his tongue moved between her lips. Dancer moved slightly, and she clung to Colt. He left her lips for a moment, keeping one arm around her as he slid off the horse and pulled her after him.

From then on they were each so possessed with passion and need that nothing else existed for them. He pulled her into the grass, and they both felt consumed by need and long-repressed desires. His kisses were hard and deep, leaving her no time to reason or to object, and hardly able to get her breath. She suspected that even if she wanted to stop him, she surely could not now. And why would she want to? This was what she had wanted for so long, what she had dreamed about for years; but it was so much more exciting and glorious than she imagined.

INTIMATE STRANGERS
by
Alexandra Thorne
author of DESERT HEAT

At thirty-two Jade Howard was facing a world of shattered dreams: once a bestselling novelist with all of Hollywood at her feet, she was now the critics' favorite target. And all she wanted was to get away. . . .

But they say you should beware of what you wish for, for in a picturesque hotel in Santa Fe, Jade will slip into a flame-colored dress—and wake up in another woman's life, with another woman's friends, her home . . . and her husband.

He is an intimate stranger, tall, dark, devastating—and hell-bent on driving his wife to adultery and divorce. It almost works . . . until Duncan Carlisle falls in love again, with the ravishing interloper he thinks is his wife. How can Jade tell him that the lady in his bed and in his heart is not who she seems? It is a risk she must take, and soon . . . before the real Megan Carlisle returns . . . before time itself tries to wrench two lovers apart.

Duncan had been riding for an hour, thinking about his lunch with Megan. He had enjoyed being with her, talking to her, listening to her, looking at her. Had a stranger walked in, he would have been convinced they were a happily married couple. God knows, Megan was trying. Could he believe what she said about wanting to start over?

She had seemed sincere.

After ten years of marriage, he thought he knew every nuance of her voice. He could usually tell when she was lying, and this time he could swear she had been telling the truth. She wanted a second chance to make their marriage work. To be perfectly honest, if she continued to act the way she had the last few days, so did he.

He reined his horse to a stop. "What do you think, Excalibur?" he asked the Arabian stallion. "Should I give Megan another chance?"

Why not? he answered himself. What did he have to lose? He turned Excalibur back toward Rancho Cielo and spurred the horse to a gallop. Half an hour later, he rode into the stable, jumped off the horse's back, unsaddled him, and although he felt guilty about putting the horse up wet, led the stallion into his stall.

Megan wasn't in the kitchen when he walked in, although she had obviously washed their lunch dishes before leaving. He expected to find her in their bedroom, but she wasn't there either. Walking back toward the living room, he heard sounds coming from the den.

Megan was seated at his desk, going through his papers. Stock certificates, canceled checks, insurance policies, and his personal correspondence lay scattered in front of her. The hopeful feeling that had swelled within him on the ride home dissolved. Anger replaced it.

"What the hell are you doing?" he asked, walking up behind her and pulling her from the chair.

The papers in her hands spilled to the floor as he spun her around to face him.

"I was just . . ."

"Just what? Trying to figure how much money you'd get if I didn't change my mind about the divorce?"

She tried to pull away but he held her fast. She had been so disarmingly sweet an hour ago. Now he realized it had just been a ruse. The bitch. She had betrayed his trust again. Rage surged in his chest as he glared down at her.

Jade wanted to look away from the fire burning in Duncan's eyes, but his fury riveted her. She didn't dare tell him why she had been snooping through his papers, yet her continued silence seemed to heighten his wrath.

Her breath caught in her throat, her pulse pounded in her ears as he gripped her harder. She could feel the heat pounding from his body, the same heat that had been so comforting in bed last night. Now she took no solace from that warmth. She feared it, feared what it was making her feel.

Duncan was magnificent in his anger. Compelling. She knew she ought to struggle, try to free herself. But her body had stopped responding to her mind. She continued to stare into his eyes, seeing pain there—and something else. Desire. God. Her stomach tightened as she realized that he wanted her.

Her arms seemed to rise of their own volition. Her fingers tangled in his hair as she pulled his head down to hers. A wildness burst into life inside her. She heard him groan, a primal sound that sent urgent messages coursing through her blood. Then her lips met his.

Duncan pulled her against him and kissed her so hard, he knew her lips would be bruised. She had used sex as a weapon before. How like her to use it now.

He wanted to punish her, to hurt her the way she had just hurt him. Instead he found himself drowning in the sweet curves that fit his body so perfectly. Her lips parted under the pressure of his kiss, and he explored her mouth with his tongue while his eager hands explored her body with rough urgency. He gripped her buttocks, forcing the swell of her stomach against him.

She was so hot. He wanted to bury himself inside her, to devour every inch of her flesh—the ruby-tipped breasts, the deep well of her navel, the generous black bush that hid the honeyed depths of her.

Her tongue found his, flaring his lust so that it burned even brighter than his anger. He felt her nipples harden through the cloth of his shirt and remembered the sweet ache of sucking them. She met his rising passion with a frenzied need of her own that implored, urged, taunted. Megan. Oh God. *Megan.*

Suddenly, without even realizing he was going to do it, he pushed her away. He wanted her, dammit, with a hunger that blasted his bones. But he'd see himself in hell before he made love to her again. An hour of pleasure wasn't worth a lifetime of misery and regret.

Jade was so weak with desire, she wasn't sure she could stand without Duncan's arms around her. She clenched her hands and locked her knees to keep from swaying, then opened her eyes wide to gaze at the man she wanted more than she had ever wanted anything or anyone. She ached to give herself to him, to yield up the secrets of her body and her soul.

Now she saw rejection plainly written on his face. She had seen that look on a man's face before, the day Paul broke their engagement. Seeing it again made her want to weep, to scream out her anguish. She wanted to fly at Duncan and rake her nails across his face, to draw blood to match the hemorrhaging wounds he'd inflicted on her soul.

But she wouldn't give him the satisfaction. Instead, she stiffened her spine and walked out of the den without a backward glance. She would have liked to keep right on walking straight out of the house, up the drive, out of Duncan Carlisle's life. But she didn't have that option.

She had never been more aroused by a man. The realization that he didn't want her, could barely stand to touch her, made her sick. Where were her pride and independence now? Trampled under his feet, that's where. Although she had never been much of a drinker, she would have gladly gotten blind drunk. She didn't have that option either.

It took all her courage, all her considerable willpower to force herself to do what she had to do. She returned to the quiet of the master bedroom and, with a calculation born of desperation, began cataloguing what she'd learned so far.

Duncan Carlisle was successful, wealthy, a gifted artist who would go down in history as the finest painter of his era. In addition he was handsome, and she now knew that, despite the coldness he often displayed with her, he was a passionate lover when he wanted to be. But she would see him in hell before she let him touch her again.

The only thing she knew about Megan was that she had a passion for clothes. It wasn't enough—not by a damn sight. Jade sat down at Megan's dressing table and looked at herself in the mirror, comparing her reflection to the woman in the photographs.

She saw the differences so clearly. Why didn't Duncan? And what had happened to Megan? Had she too passed through the door to time? Was Aurora the key? Was it the dress? Or was it some unforeseen combination of circumstances that might never happen again?

She knew nothing about time-travel theories, except that it was a popular topic in science-fiction novels. Perhaps serious books had been written about the possibility, though. Perhaps in the Sante Fe library . . . No. She rejected the idea. From what she recalled, Einstein had just developed his space-time theory. A local library wasn't going to be any help.

Her shoulders sagged. She sighed heavily. She was stuck here, trapped in another woman's life, sleeping with her husband. And she had to face it. Part of her wanted to stay.

She opened the top drawer of the dressing table. Megan's cosmetics filled it, and she began applying them, as if she could absorb the other woman's personality through her pores. When she finished, she studied herself in the mirror again. That was better. The makeup did make her look more like Megan. But what good would that do unless she could think and act like her as well?

She simply had no choice. She would have to tell Duncan the truth tonight. Grimacing at the possible consequences, she idly opened the bottom drawer where Megan kept her jewels. Dazzled by the array, she picked up the velvet-lined tray and put it on her lap. She was about to shut the drawer when she realized the tray had covered a series of slender leather-bound books. Bending down for a closer look, she saw each one was stamped with a year, beginning with 1919 and ending with 1929. They had to be Megan's diaries.

Bingo, she exulted, and picked up the first volume.

LIGHTNING
by Patricia Potter
author of
LAWLESS and RAINBOW

LIGHTNING is a lush, dramatic, and truly emotional historical romance, set during the Civil War. Lauren Bradley was the new coquette in the tropical port of Nassau. Only the kindly shopkeeper knew the beautiful young woman had agreed to avenge her brother's death by becoming a Yankee spy in this stronghold of Confederate blockade runners.

Englishman Adrian Cabot was the most daring of those who ran supplies to the South. As handsome as sin and fearless as the devil, he had sworn to recover his family's honor with the profits from his dangerous missions. No one knew of the need that burned within him—except Lauren, who heard in his bold laughter the sound of a wounded soul.

Their meeting was fated. She was sent by Washington to sabotage his ship. He was sent by destiny to steal her heart. Together on board the Specter, *they were swept into passion's treacherous sea, tasting deeply of ecstasy and the danger of war.*

In the following scene, Lauren and Adrian are aboard the Specter, *the engines of which she plans to sabotage. Her discovery that Adrian has made a wager with another captain over who would first win her affection steels her resolve to stop his blockade running. . . .*

"Lauren." Adrian's voice was soft in her ear, and she returned to the moment, to the seductive night, and the danger. His danger. Her own danger when she was with him. Dear God, how could she survive this?

Hate him, she urged herself. Hate him for what he is, for what he's doing, for what he wagered.

But that was like hating the warm, bright sun, hating the brightness while the body drank up the warmth.

"Frightened?" he said, his hand on her shoulder tightening ever so slightly.

Lauren kept her gaze away from him. She couldn't look at him now, as the eyes so deep a blue she could never find its source, or identify the currents that ran in them. She didn't understand him, or the many contradictions she saw in him.

"Yes," she said. But not for the reason he believed.

"The run is really fairly safe," he said, leaning over, his words a soft whisper in the night as his breath touched her ear, and she shivered.

His hand dropped from her shoulder, and both of his arms went around her waist. She found herself leaning back against him. It was so natural, as if it was meant to be, this fusing of bodies.

The lamps on the ship were quenched, one by one, and she turned, looking askance at him in a night now lit only by a host of stars that were bright in the sky but flashed precious little light to the earth.

"It's time," he whispered, "to get lost in the night."

Lauren watched as distant lights also disappeared, one by one, and she and Adrian seemed alone in the total blackness of night. Even the loud voices of the crew had quieted to whispers, and only the sound of water against the hull made music in the vast emptiness.

The sudden void matched the hollowness inside her. Adrian's arms were still around her, and something deep inside her relished the comfort of his embrace. But it was all false, she reminded herself. He doesn't mean it, any more than she did.

She forced some words out. "Isn't it dangerous . . . without lights?"

"Johnny's the best pilot in the business. He can sense—see—every reef, every jut of land in the blackest of nights. Damned if I know how. Part owl, I suppose."

Keep talking. Keep talking so you won't feel. Lauren shifted slightly, and Adrian's arms moved with her. The friction of skin against skin, body against body, sent waves of painful pleasure washing over her. She wanted his hands to move again, to reexperience those wonderful sensations that made her feel so alive.

There was a tug on her skirt, and she looked down, barely able to see Socrates in the darkness. Then she tipped her head upward. The shadow of Adrian's head, the outline of those hard, clean features so close, came even closer as she felt his lips touch her cheek and his hands turn her ever so slightly so she was at his side rather than in front of him.

Her heart thumped so loudly she thought he must hear. Her hand trembled when it lay on the railing. His lips moved to touch her lips, softly, searchingly.

Lauren knew they were lost in the shadow, in the inky darkness, so the members of the crew could not see. It was as if they were alone in an infinite empty vault, nothing real except each other. She felt his lips press tighter against her mouth, and she realized she was responding, her mouth opening to his gentle probing.

Emotions flooded her. Wild, runaway emotions. Pleasure. Need. Anticipation. The danger, the tension, made everything so much more intense, magnified her sensations until she didn't know how she could bear them, to hold them inside without exploding. She was learning quickly what Adrian had meant about danger.

Or was it the danger?

She stepped back frantically. "No," she whispered, and his arms loosened from around her. His lips whispered against her cheek, and then his hand caught her chin, making her look up at him. She couldn't see his features well, but in her mind she saw his slight smile, the question in his eyes.

"You're like quicksilver, Miss Bradley," he said softly. "You keep running away from me. Why?"

Because I hate you. And I'm so afraid I also love you.

"I'm tired," she said aloud, her voice unsteady.

Adrian sighed. His head started to lower again, and Lauren knew he meant to kiss her, to kiss away her rejection, but she spun away, afraid that he would do just that.

"Please, Adrian."

"We'll talk tomorrow," he said, his voice suddenly hard and uncompromising, and she knew she was going to need to give some explanations the next day. She knew he must be totally confused, the way she yielded one moment and ran the next. The good Lord knew she was confused!

"I'll walk you to the cabin," he said, his hands leaving her as he stooped down and swept up Socrates. Adrian's right hand took her arm firmly, guiding her through the dark night air to the steps that led down to the cabin. The interior was even darker than the deck, and she wondered how he stepped so surely. She felt totally blind, completely at his mercy.

The engines hummed as Adrian's hand steadied her uncertain steps, his warmth and scent intoxicating in the cocoon of the ship, of the night. She stumbled, and his arm went around her again, keeping her from falling. Lauren felt as if he were an integral part of her, and she knew she would never be whole again when he was gone.

When he was gone!

And then they were at the cabin, and he'd opened the door. He released her, and she heard the sound of a match striking, and the flare of a lantern. "It's safe to use a light in here," he said. "There are no windows."

The lantern, really a strange-looking oil lamp designed specifically for ships, was hung from a hook, its flickering flame sending darts of light around the cabin, illuminating his face. There were so many questions in his expression—questions she could never answer.

Socrates jumped to the floor and went over to his bed.

"I'll take him with me," Adrian said.

"Why don't you leave him here?"

"Are you quite sure about that?" Adrian's voice was now tinged with amusement. "Sometimes he decides he prefers the bed. You might wake up with a bony paw clutching at you."

"At least he'll be company."

His eyes sparkled, the deep blue of them catching fire from the flame. "I find myself jealous. And of a monkey. I'll have no pride left, Miss Bradley," he teased.

"I think that unlikely," she retorted.

"You do unprecedented damage to it."

"I believe you will recover."

"Doubtful." An endearingly wistful smile played over his face. Another ploy? "Good night, Captain."

"Adrian," he insisted.

"Lord Adrian," she said, trying to keep a certain distance.

"Lord Ridgely to be correct," he said dryly. "You sound as if you dislike lords?"

"I've heard they play games," she charged unwisely.

"What kind of games?"

"With hearts." *With my heart.*

He was silent, his eyes dark and secretive, a muscle twitching in his cheek. She wished she knew why.

"Don't they?"

"Not all of them. Do all woman play games?" There was a sudden harsh edge to his voice.

Drat the man. He had a way of putting her on the defensive. Of turning her words against her. And he had wagered on her! Her anger rose again, protecting her from her own weakness. But she knew she had to guard against that too. She had already said too much. But the skin where he'd touched her still tingled, still burned, and she knew if he kissed her, she would be lost again.

She prayed briefly, and her prayers were answered. His voice low, rumbling through her consciousness, made her reply unnecessary.

"I have to get up on deck. These waters are still dangerous. Good night . . . Lauren."

There was an unusual curtness to his words, and she felt a now-familiar pain stab through her. If his censure hurt now, dear God, how much was it going to hurt when he learned the truth?